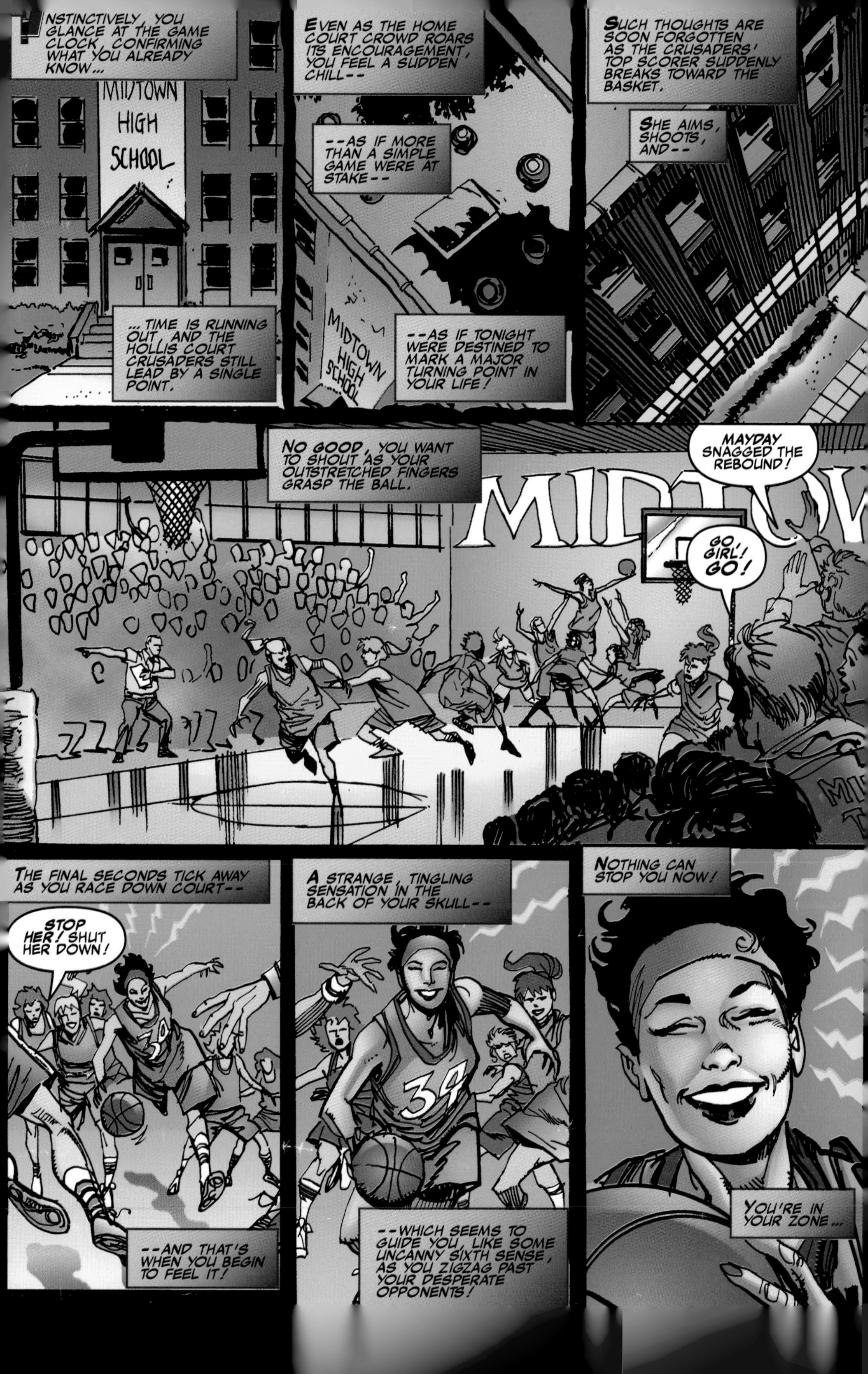
INSTINCTIVELY, YOU GLANCE AT THE GAME CLOCK, CONFIRMING WHAT YOU ALREADY KNOW...
MIDTOWN HIGH SCHOOL
...TIME IS RUNNING OUT, AND THE HOLLIS COURT CRUSADERS STILL LEAD BY A SINGLE POINT.
EVEN AS THE HOME COURT CROWD ROARS ITS ENCOURAGEMENT, YOU FEEL A SUDDEN CHILL--
--AS IF MORE THAN A SIMPLE GAME WERE AT STAKE--
MIDTOWN HIGH SCHOOL
--AS IF TONIGHT WERE DESTINED TO MARK A MAJOR TURNING POINT IN YOUR LIFE!
SUCH THOUGHTS ARE SOON FORGOTTEN AS THE CRUSADERS' TOP SCORER SUDDENLY BREAKS TOWARD THE BASKET.
SHE AIMS, SHOOTS, AND--
NO GOOD, YOU WANT TO SHOUT AS YOUR OUTSTRETCHED FINGERS GRASP THE BALL.
MAYDAY SNAGGED THE REBOUND!
GO, GIRL! GO!
THE FINAL SECONDS TICK AWAY AS YOU RACE DOWN COURT--
STOP HER! SHUT HER DOWN!
--AND THAT'S WHEN YOU BEGIN TO FEEL IT!
A STRANGE, TINGLING SENSATION IN THE BACK OF YOUR SKULL--
--WHICH SEEMS TO GUIDE YOU, LIKE SOME UNCANNY SIXTH SENSE, AS YOU ZIGZAG PAST YOUR DESPERATE OPPONENTS!
NOTHING CAN STOP YOU NOW!
YOU'RE IN YOUR ZONE...

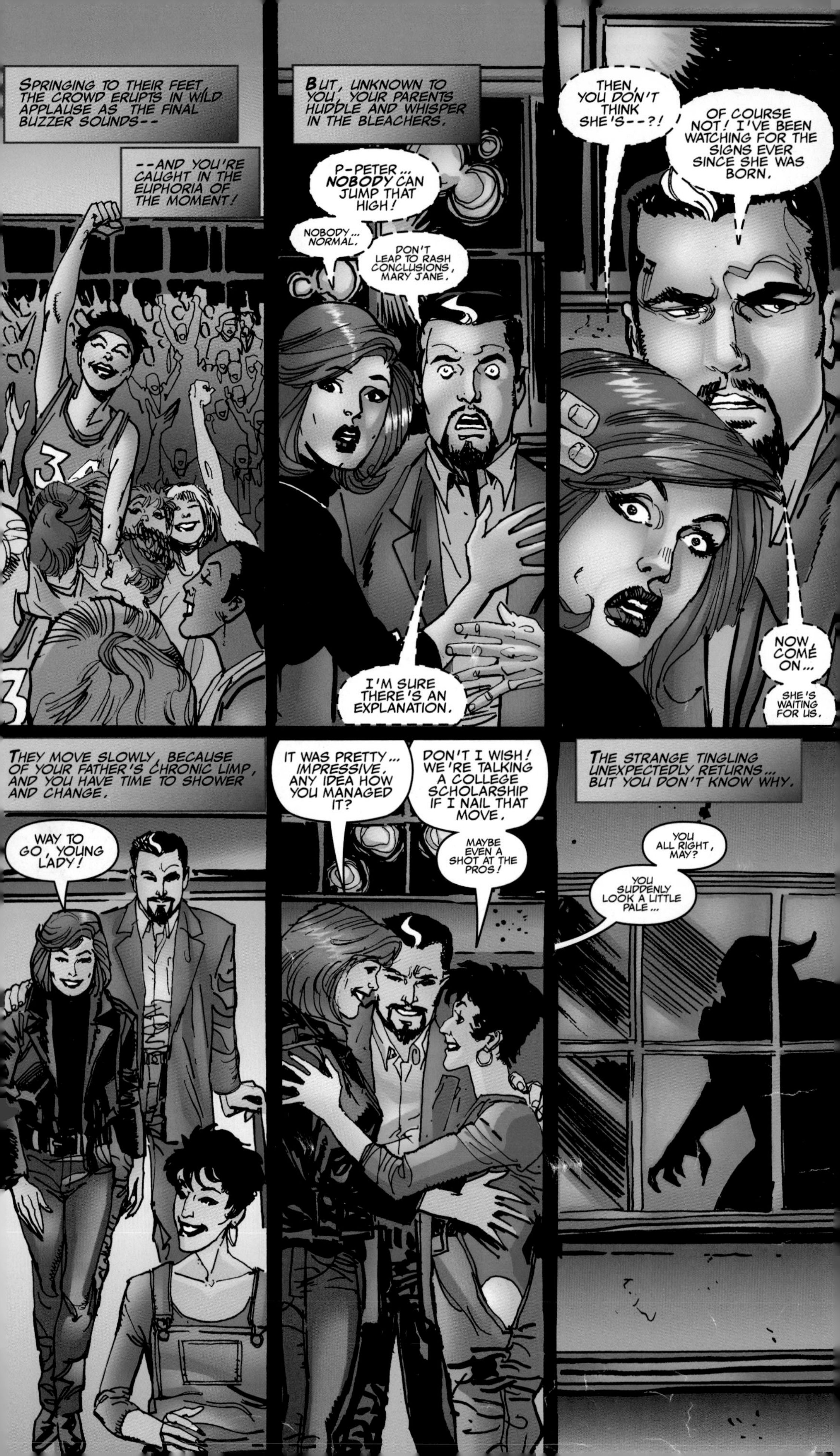

SPRINGING TO THEIR FEET, THE CROWD ERUPTS IN WILD APPLAUSE AS THE FINAL BUZZER SOUNDS--
--AND YOU'RE CAUGHT IN THE EUPHORIA OF THE MOMENT!
BUT, UNKNOWN TO YOU, YOUR PARENTS HUDDLE AND WHISPER IN THE BLEACHERS.
P-PETER... NOBODY CAN JUMP THAT HIGH!
NOBODY... NORMAL.
DON'T LEAP TO RASH CONCLUSIONS, MARY JANE.
I'M SURE THERE'S AN EXPLANATION.
THEN, YOU DON'T THINK SHE'S--?!
OF COURSE NOT! I'VE BEEN WATCHING FOR THE SIGNS EVER SINCE SHE WAS BORN.
NOW, COME ON...
SHE'S WAITING FOR US.
THEY MOVE SLOWLY, BECAUSE OF YOUR FATHER'S CHRONIC LIMP, AND YOU HAVE TIME TO SHOWER AND CHANGE.
WAY TO GO, YOUNG LADY!
IT WAS PRETTY... IMPRESSIVE. ANY IDEA HOW YOU MANAGED IT?
DON'T I WISH! WE'RE TALKING A COLLEGE SCHOLARSHIP IF I NAIL THAT MOVE.
MAYBE EVEN A SHOT AT THE PROS!
THE STRANGE TINGLING UNEXPECTEDLY RETURNS... BUT YOU DON'T KNOW WHY.
YOU ALL RIGHT, MAY?
YOU SUDDENLY LOOK A LITTLE PALE...

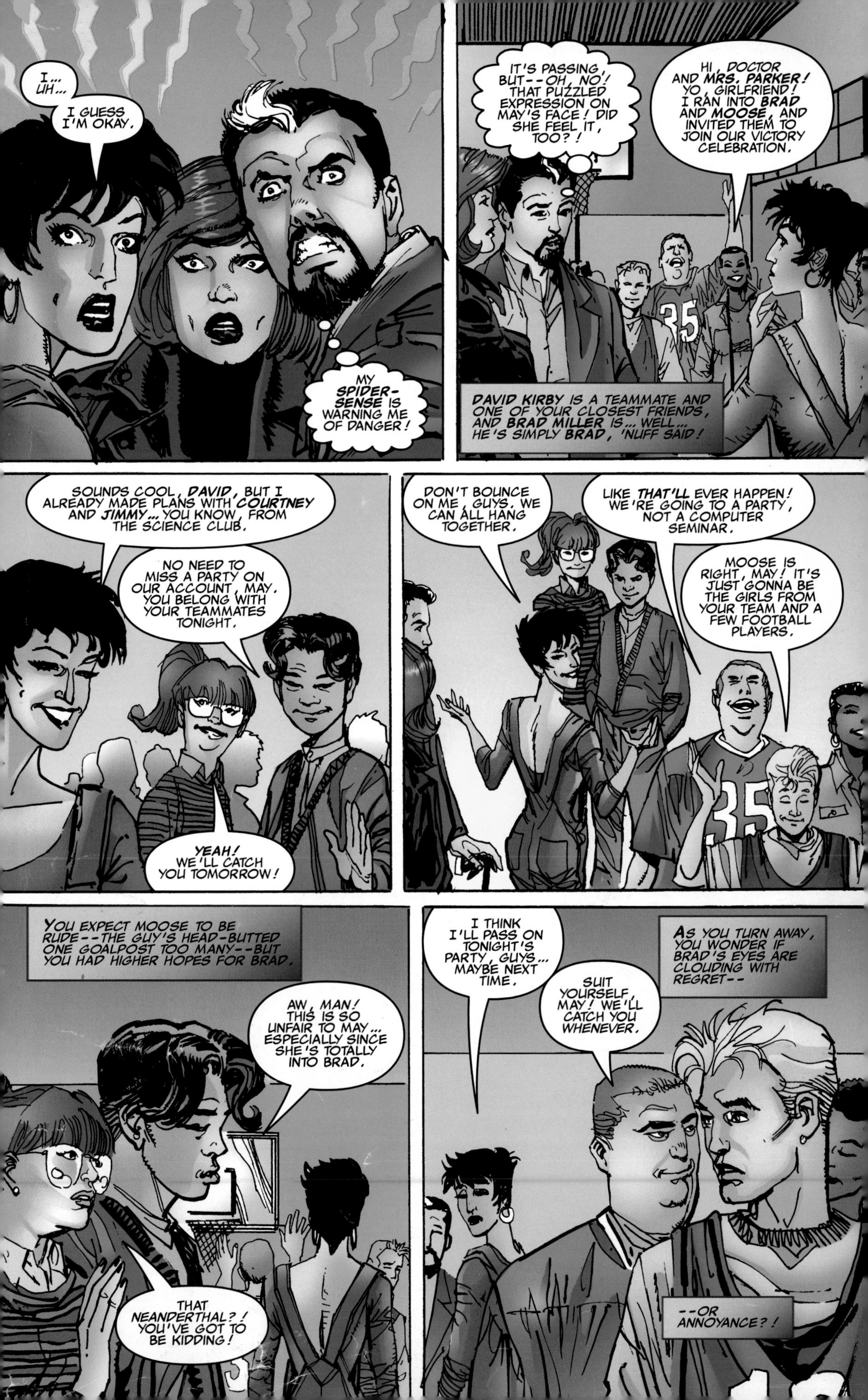
I... UH...
I GUESS I'M OKAY.
MY SPIDER-SENSE IS WARNING ME OF DANGER!
IT'S PASSING, BUT--OH, NO! THAT PUZZLED EXPRESSION ON MAY'S FACE! DID SHE FEEL IT, TOO?!
HI, DOCTOR AND MRS. PARKER! YO, GIRLFRIEND! I RAN INTO BRAD AND MOOSE, AND INVITED THEM TO JOIN OUR VICTORY CELEBRATION.
DAVID KIRBY IS A TEAMMATE AND ONE OF YOUR CLOSEST FRIENDS, AND BRAD MILLER IS... WELL... HE'S SIMPLY BRAD, 'NUFF SAID!
SOUNDS COOL, DAVID, BUT I ALREADY MADE PLANS WITH COURTNEY AND JIMMY... YOU KNOW, FROM THE SCIENCE CLUB.
NO NEED TO MISS A PARTY ON OUR ACCOUNT, MAY. YOU BELONG WITH YOUR TEAMMATES TONIGHT.
YEAH! WE'LL CATCH YOU TOMORROW!
DON'T BOUNCE ON ME, GUYS. WE CAN ALL HANG TOGETHER.
LIKE THAT'LL EVER HAPPEN! WE'RE GOING TO A PARTY, NOT A COMPUTER SEMINAR.
MOOSE IS RIGHT, MAY! IT'S JUST GONNA BE THE GIRLS FROM YOUR TEAM AND A FEW FOOTBALL PLAYERS.
YOU EXPECT MOOSE TO BE RUDE--THE GUY'S HEAD-BUTTED ONE GOALPOST TOO MANY--BUT YOU HAD HIGHER HOPES FOR BRAD.
AW, MAN! THIS IS SO UNFAIR TO MAY... ESPECIALLY SINCE SHE'S TOTALLY INTO BRAD.
THAT NEANDERTHAL?! YOU'VE GOT TO BE KIDDING!
I THINK I'LL PASS ON TONIGHT'S PARTY, GUYS... MAYBE NEXT TIME.
SUIT YOURSELF, MAY! WE'LL CATCH YOU WHENEVER.
AS YOU TURN AWAY, YOU WONDER IF BRAD'S EYES ARE CLOUDING WITH REGRET--
--OR ANNOYANCE?!

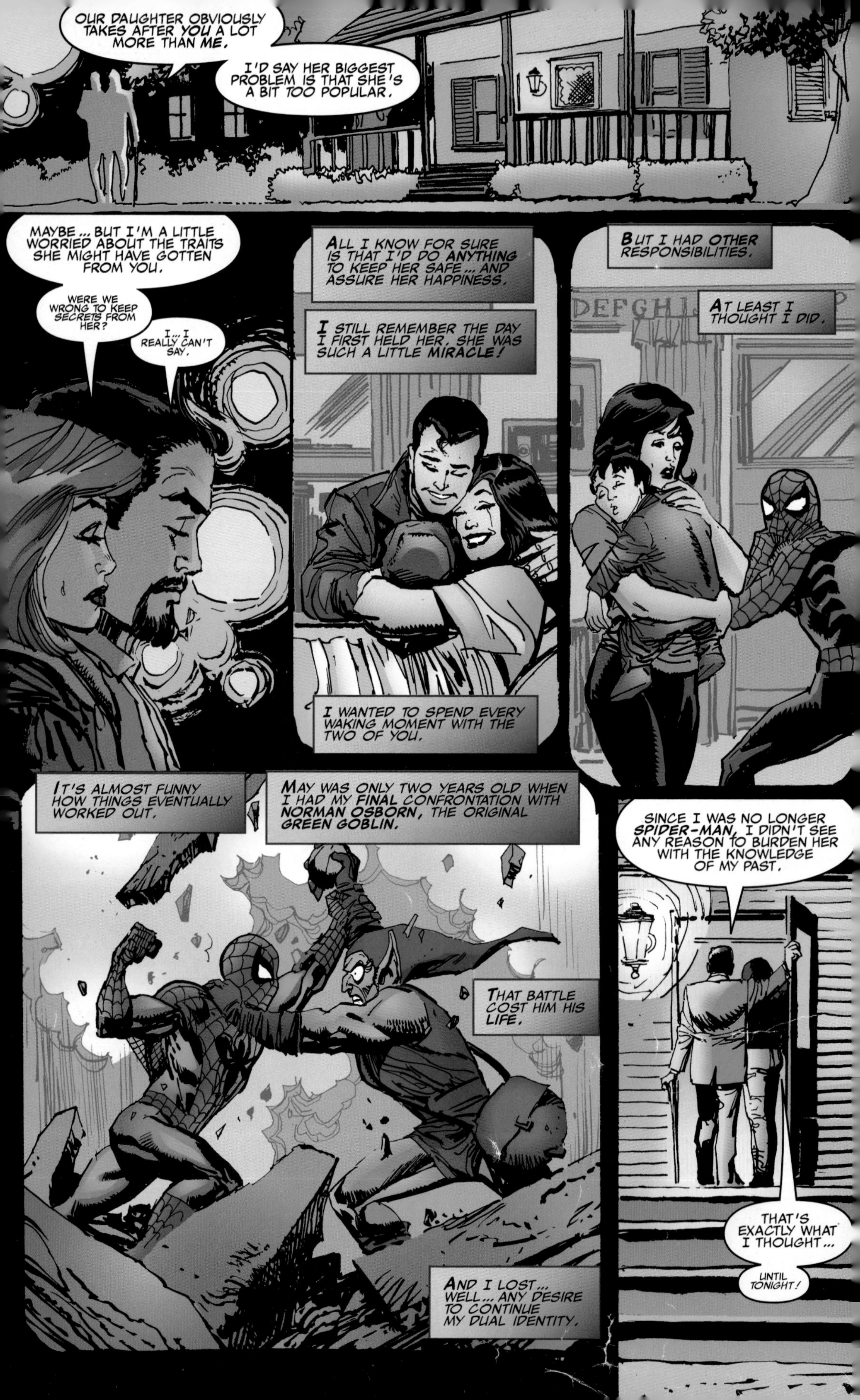
OUR DAUGHTER OBVIOUSLY TAKES AFTER YOU A LOT MORE THAN ME.
I'D SAY HER BIGGEST PROBLEM IS THAT SHE'S A BIT TOO POPULAR.
MAYBE ... BUT I'M A LITTLE WORRIED ABOUT THE TRAITS SHE MIGHT HAVE GOTTEN FROM YOU.
WERE WE WRONG TO KEEP SECRETS FROM HER?
I... I REALLY CAN'T SAY.
ALL I KNOW FOR SURE IS THAT I'D DO ANYTHING TO KEEP HER SAFE... AND ASSURE HER HAPPINESS.
I STILL REMEMBER THE DAY I FIRST HELD HER. SHE WAS SUCH A LITTLE MIRACLE!
I WANTED TO SPEND EVERY WAKING MOMENT WITH THE TWO OF YOU.
BUT I HAD OTHER RESPONSIBILITIES.
AT LEAST I THOUGHT I DID.
IT'S ALMOST FUNNY HOW THINGS EVENTUALLY WORKED OUT.
MAY WAS ONLY TWO YEARS OLD WHEN I HAD MY FINAL CONFRONTATION WITH NORMAN OSBORN, THE ORIGINAL GREEN GOBLIN.
THAT BATTLE COST HIM HIS LIFE.
AND I LOST... WELL... ANY DESIRE TO CONTINUE MY DUAL IDENTITY.
SINCE I WAS NO LONGER SPIDER-MAN, I DIDN'T SEE ANY REASON TO BURDEN HER WITH THE KNOWLEDGE OF MY PAST.
THAT'S EXACTLY WHAT I THOUGHT...
UNTIL TONIGHT!

VISIT US AT

www.abdopub.com

Spotlight, a division of ABDO Publishing Company Inc., is the school and library distributor of the Marvel Entertainment books.

Library bound edition © 2006

Library of Congress Cataloging-in-Publication Data

Legacy...In Black and White

ISBN 1-59961-029-9   (Reinforced Library Bound Edition)

All Spotlight books are reinforced library binding and manufactured in the United States of America

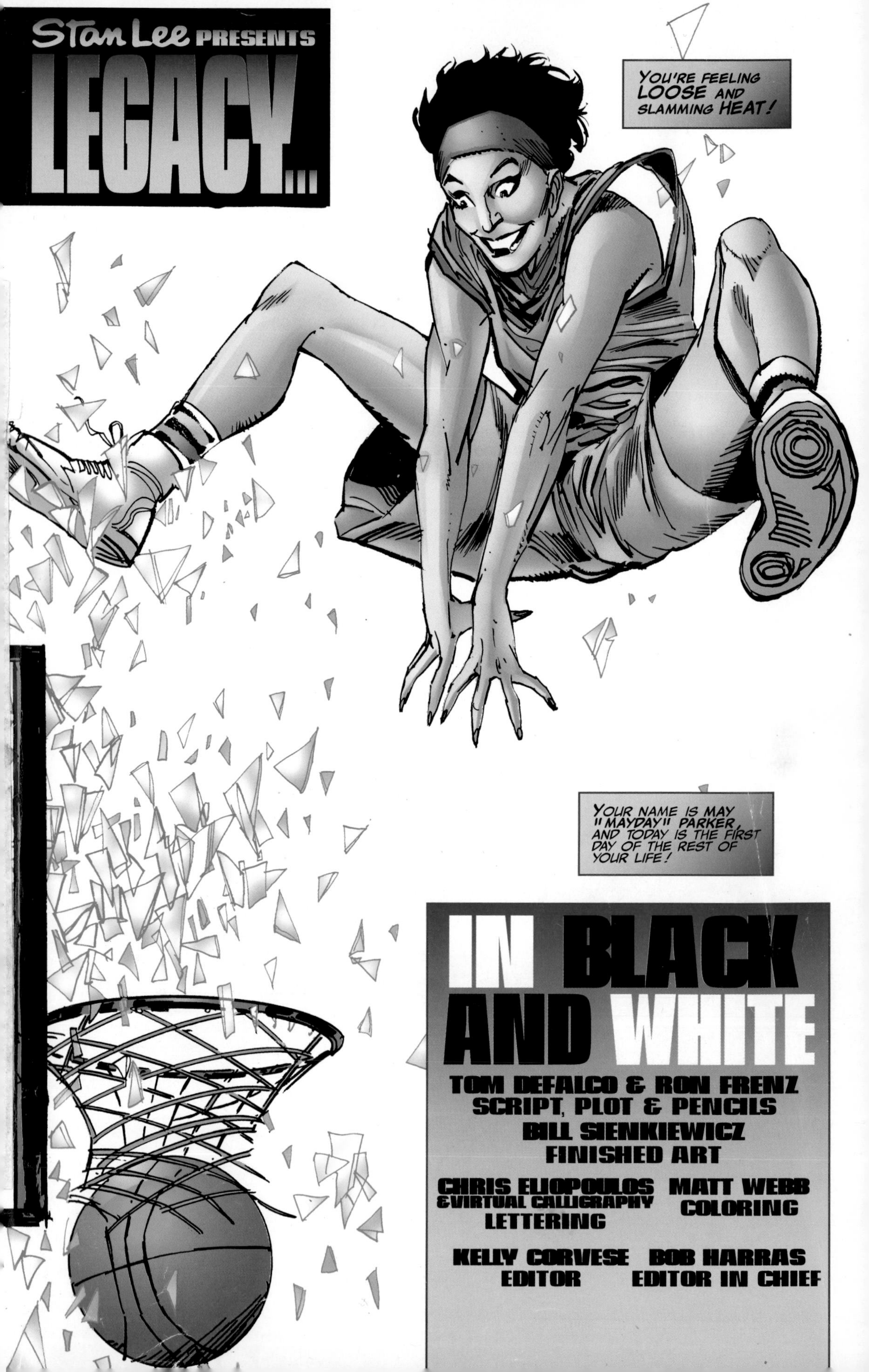
STAN LEE PRESENTS
LEGACY...
YOU'RE FEELING LOOSE AND SLAMMING HEAT!
YOUR NAME IS MAY "MAYDAY" PARKER, AND TODAY IS THE FIRST DAY OF THE REST OF YOUR LIFE!
IN BLACK AND WHITE
TOM DEFALCO & RON FRENZ
SCRIPT, PLOT & PENCILS
BILL SIENKIEWICZ
FINISHED ART
CHRIS ELIOPOULOS &VIRTUAL CALLIGRAPHY
LETTERING
MATT WEBB
COLORING
KELLY CORVESE
EDITOR
BOB HARRAS
EDITOR IN CHIEF

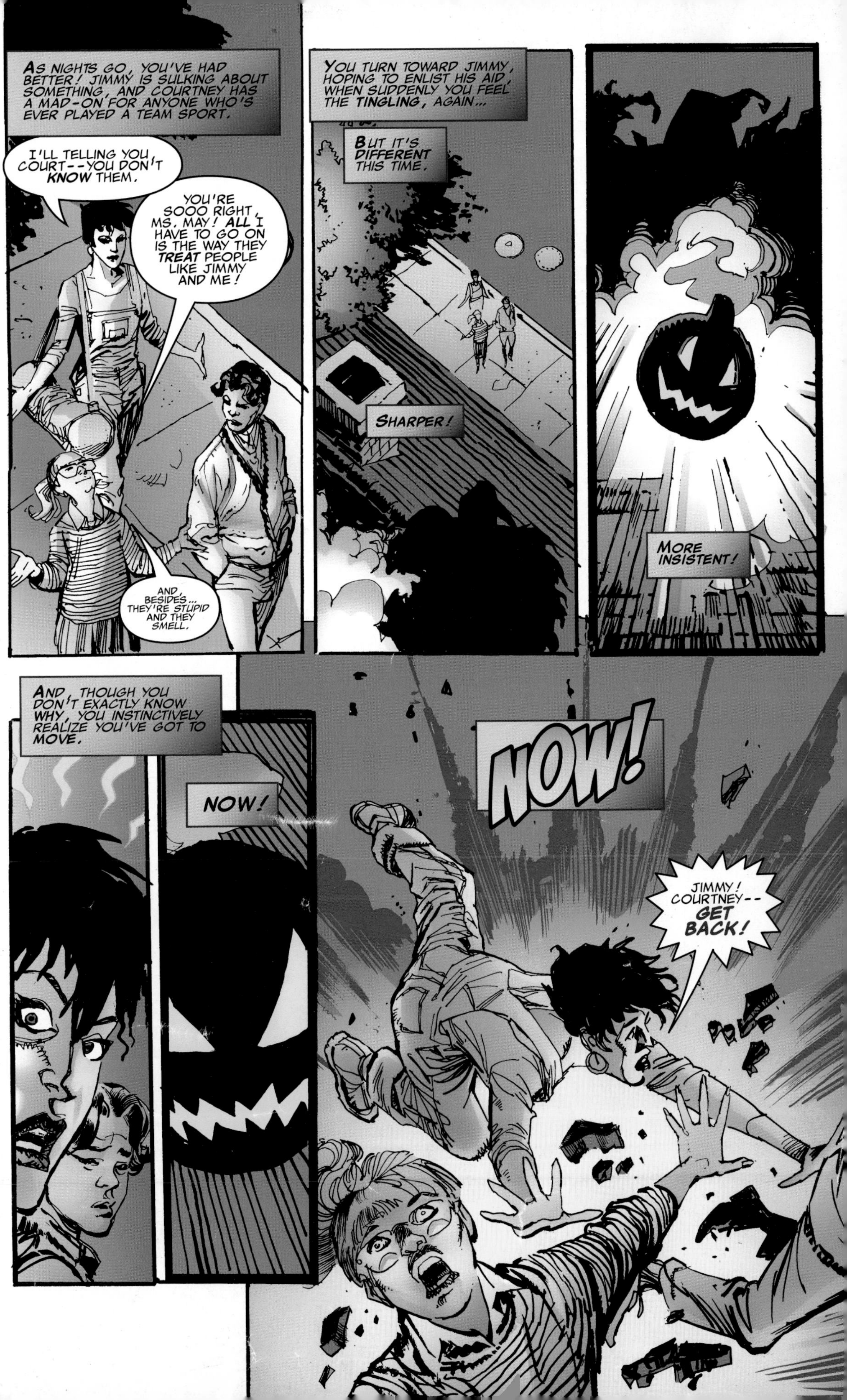

As nights go, you've had better! Jimmy is sulking about something, and Courtney has a mad-on for anyone who's ever played a team sport.
I'll telling you, Court--you don't know them.
You're sooo right, Ms. May! All I have to go on is the way they treat people like Jimmy and me!
And, besides... they're stupid and they smell.
You turn toward Jimmy, hoping to enlist his aid, when suddenly you feel the tingling, again...
But it's different this time.
Sharper!
More insistent!
And, though you don't exactly know why, you instinctively realize you've got to move.
Now!
NOW!
Jimmy! Courtney--get back!

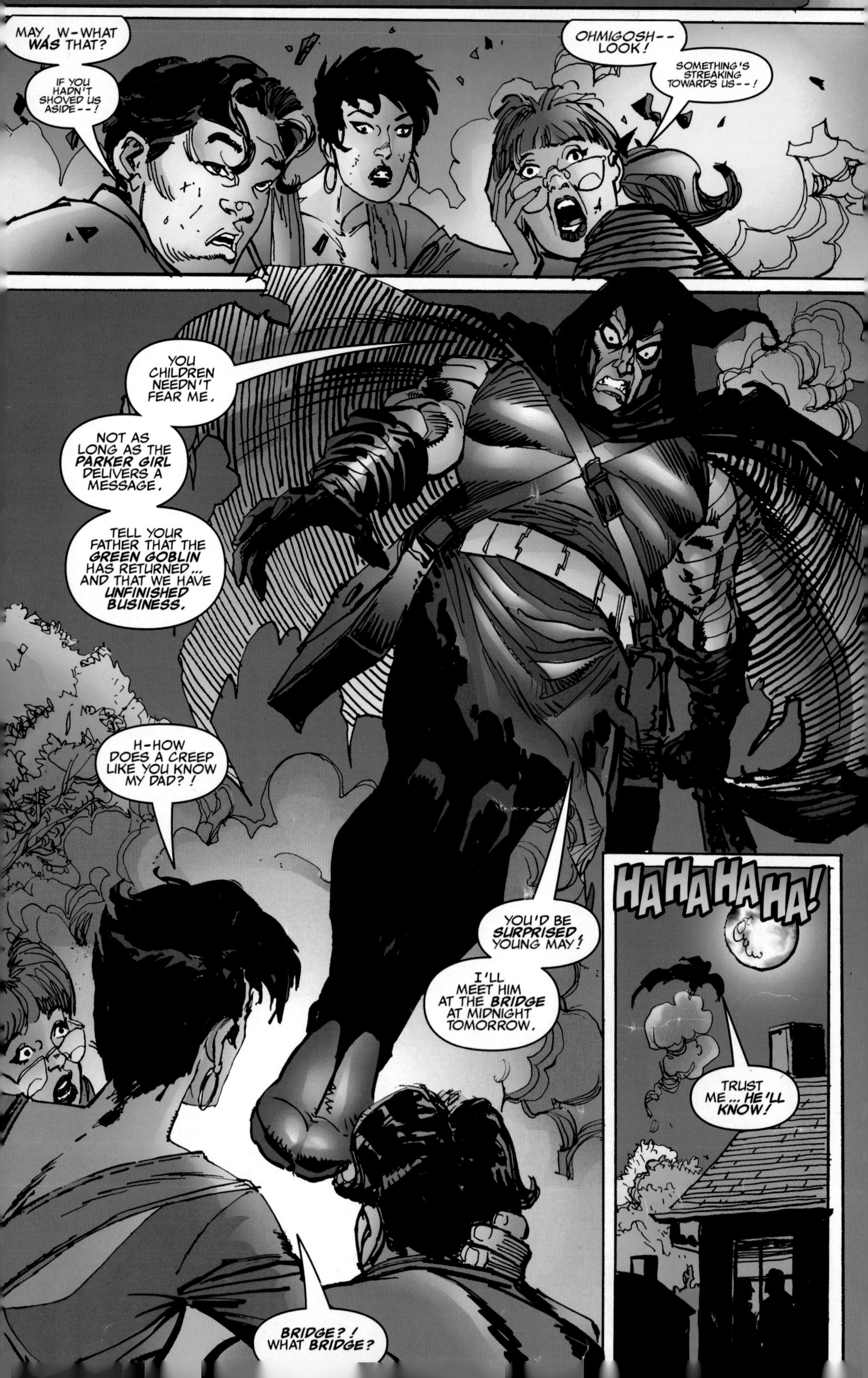
MAY, W-WHAT WAS THAT?
IF YOU HADN'T SHOVED US ASIDE--!
OHMIGOSH--LOOK!
SOMETHING'S STREAKING TOWARDS US--!
YOU CHILDREN NEEDN'T FEAR ME.
NOT AS LONG AS THE PARKER GIRL DELIVERS A MESSAGE.
TELL YOUR FATHER THAT THE GREEN GOBLIN HAS RETURNED... AND THAT WE HAVE UNFINISHED BUSINESS.
H-HOW DOES A CREEP LIKE YOU KNOW MY DAD?!
YOU'D BE SURPRISED, YOUNG MAY!
I'LL MEET HIM AT THE BRIDGE AT MIDNIGHT TOMORROW.
BRIDGE?! WHAT BRIDGE?
HA HA HA HA HA!
TRUST ME... HE'LL KNOW!

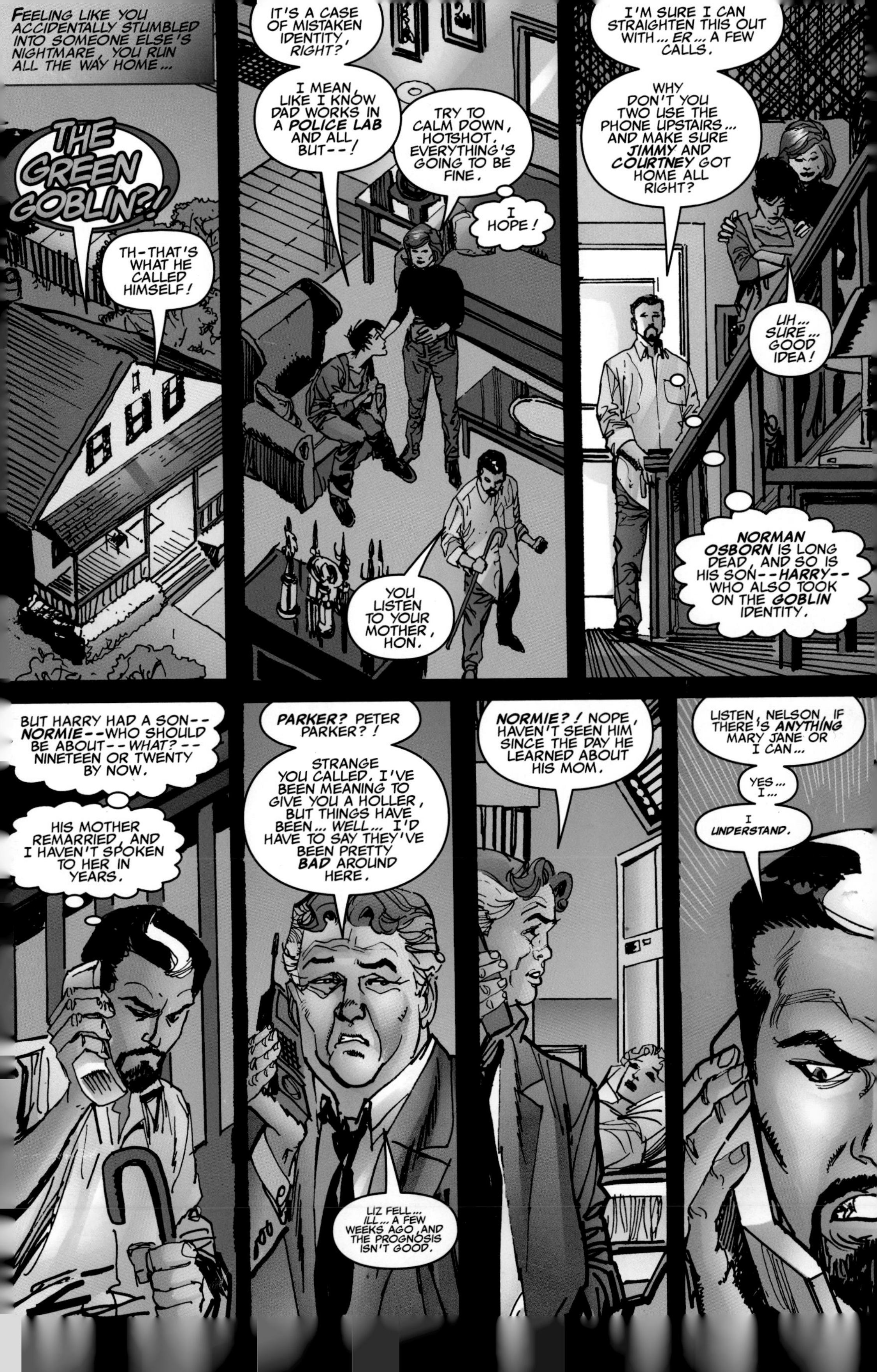
FEELING LIKE YOU ACCIDENTALLY STUMBLED INTO SOMEONE ELSE'S NIGHTMARE, YOU RUN ALL THE WAY HOME...
THE GREEN GOBLIN?!
TH-THAT'S WHAT HE CALLED HIMSELF!
IT'S A CASE OF MISTAKEN IDENTITY, RIGHT?
I MEAN, LIKE I KNOW DAD WORKS IN A POLICE LAB AND ALL, BUT--!
TRY TO CALM DOWN, HOTSHOT. EVERYTHING'S GOING TO BE FINE.
I HOPE!
YOU LISTEN TO YOUR MOTHER, HON.
I'M SURE I CAN STRAIGHTEN THIS OUT WITH... ER... A FEW CALLS.
WHY DON'T YOU TWO USE THE PHONE UPSTAIRS... AND MAKE SURE JIMMY AND COURTNEY GOT HOME ALL RIGHT?
UH... SURE... GOOD IDEA!
NORMAN OSBORN IS LONG DEAD, AND SO IS HIS SON--HARRY--WHO ALSO TOOK ON THE GOBLIN IDENTITY.
BUT HARRY HAD A SON--NORMIE--WHO SHOULD BE ABOUT--WHAT?--NINETEEN OR TWENTY BY NOW.
HIS MOTHER REMARRIED, AND I HAVEN'T SPOKEN TO HER IN YEARS.
PARKER? PETER PARKER?!
STRANGE YOU CALLED. I'VE BEEN MEANING TO GIVE YOU A HOLLER, BUT THINGS HAVE BEEN... WELL... I'D HAVE TO SAY THEY'VE BEEN PRETTY BAD AROUND HERE.
LIZ FELL... ILL... A FEW WEEKS AGO, AND THE PROGNOSIS ISN'T GOOD.
NORMIE?! NOPE, HAVEN'T SEEN HIM SINCE THE DAY HE LEARNED ABOUT HIS MOM.
LISTEN, NELSON, IF THERE'S ANYTHING MARY JANE OR I CAN...
YES... I...
I UNDERSTAND.

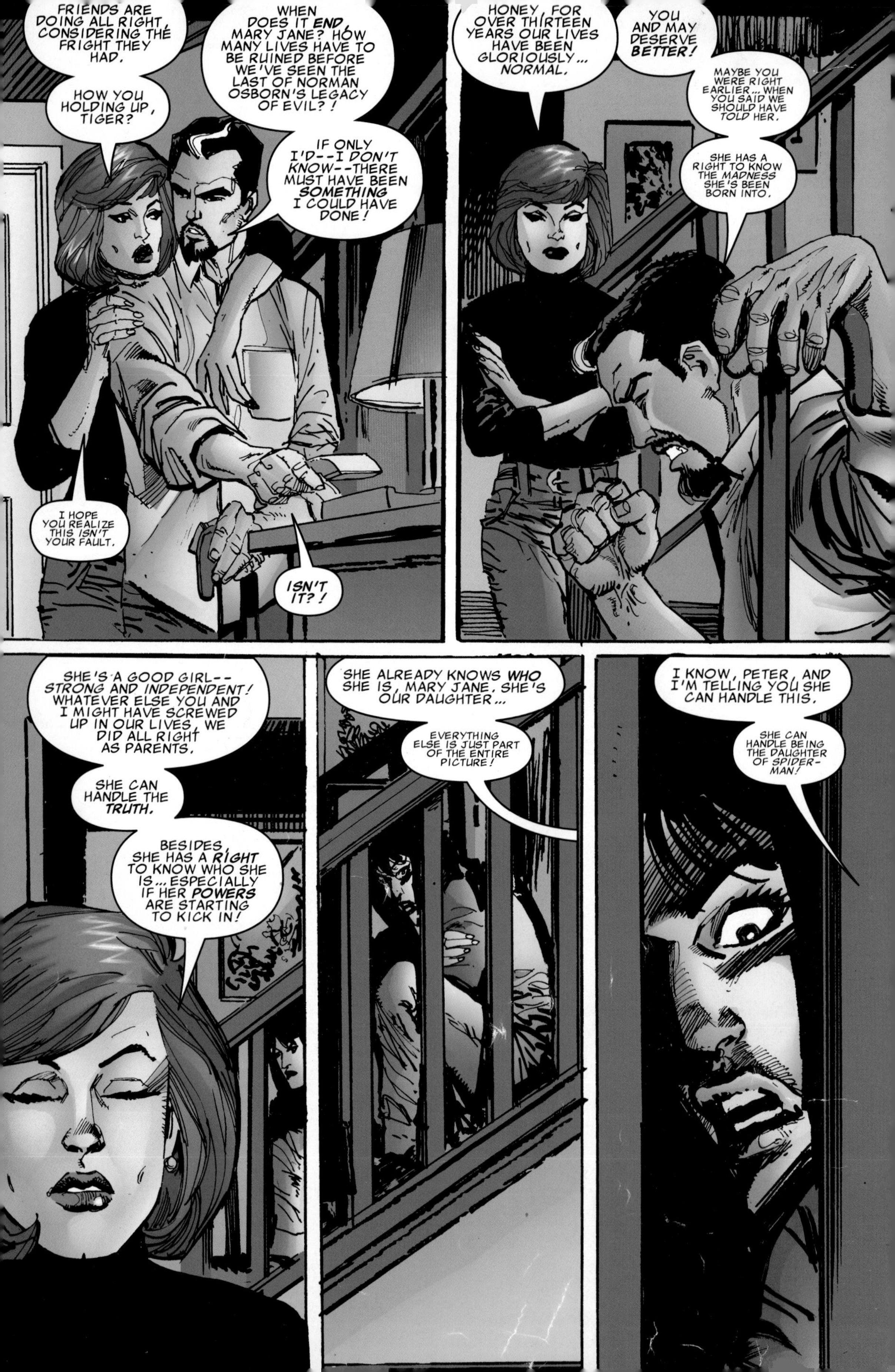
FRIENDS ARE DOING ALL RIGHT, CONSIDERING THE FRIGHT THEY HAD.
HOW YOU HOLDING UP, TIGER?
WHEN DOES IT END, MARY JANE? HOW MANY LIVES HAVE TO BE RUINED BEFORE WE'VE SEEN THE LAST OF NORMAN OSBORN'S LEGACY OF EVIL?!
IF ONLY I'D--I DON'T KNOW--THERE MUST HAVE BEEN SOMETHING I COULD HAVE DONE!
I HOPE YOU REALIZE THIS ISN'T YOUR FAULT.
ISN'T IT?!
HONEY, FOR OVER THIRTEEN YEARS OUR LIVES HAVE BEEN GLORIOUSLY... NORMAL.
YOU AND MAY DESERVE BETTER!
MAYBE YOU WERE RIGHT EARLIER... WHEN YOU SAID WE SHOULD HAVE TOLD HER.
SHE HAS A RIGHT TO KNOW THE MADNESS SHE'S BEEN BORN INTO.
SHE'S A GOOD GIRL--STRONG AND INDEPENDENT! WHATEVER ELSE YOU AND I MIGHT HAVE SCREWED UP IN OUR LIVES, WE DID ALL RIGHT AS PARENTS.
SHE CAN HANDLE THE TRUTH.
BESIDES, SHE HAS A RIGHT TO KNOW WHO SHE IS... ESPECIALLY IF HER POWERS ARE STARTING TO KICK IN!
SHE ALREADY KNOWS WHO SHE IS, MARY JANE. SHE'S OUR DAUGHTER...
EVERYTHING ELSE IS JUST PART OF THE ENTIRE PICTURE!
I KNOW, PETER, AND I'M TELLING YOU SHE CAN HANDLE THIS.
SHE CAN HANDLE BEING THE DAUGHTER OF SPIDER-MAN!

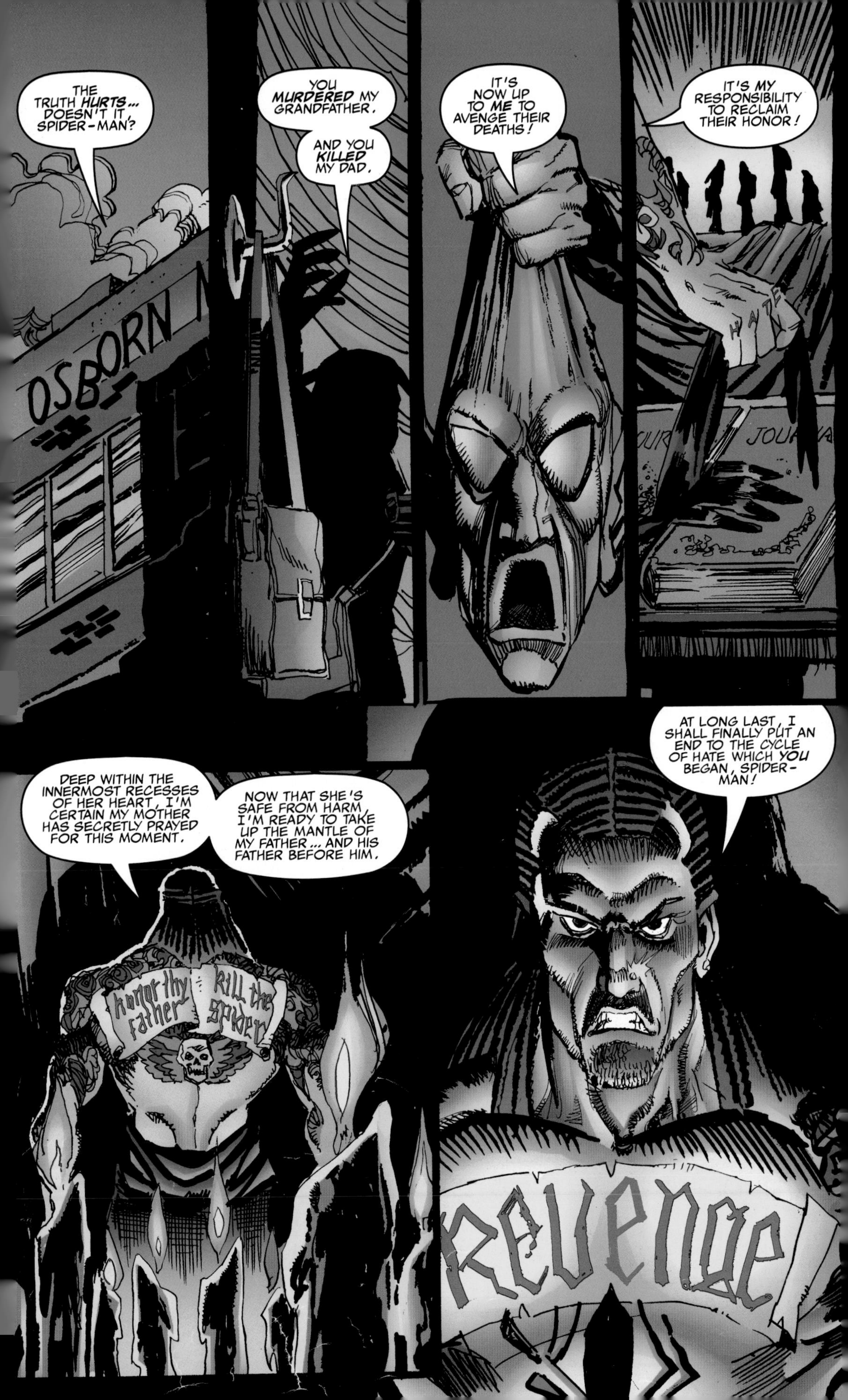
THE TRUTH HURTS... DOESN'T IT, SPIDER-MAN?
OSBORN
YOU MURDERED MY GRANDFATHER.
AND YOU KILLED MY DAD.
IT'S NOW UP TO ME TO AVENGE THEIR DEATHS!
IT'S MY RESPONSIBILITY TO RECLAIM THEIR HONOR!
HATE
JOURNAL
DEEP WITHIN THE INNERMOST RECESSES OF HER HEART, I'M CERTAIN MY MOTHER HAS SECRETLY PRAYED FOR THIS MOMENT.
NOW THAT SHE'S SAFE FROM HARM, I'M READY TO TAKE UP THE MANTLE OF MY FATHER... AND HIS FATHER BEFORE HIM.
honor thy father
kill the spider
AT LONG LAST, I SHALL FINALLY PUT AN END TO THE CYCLE OF HATE WHICH YOU BEGAN, SPIDER-MAN!
REVENGE

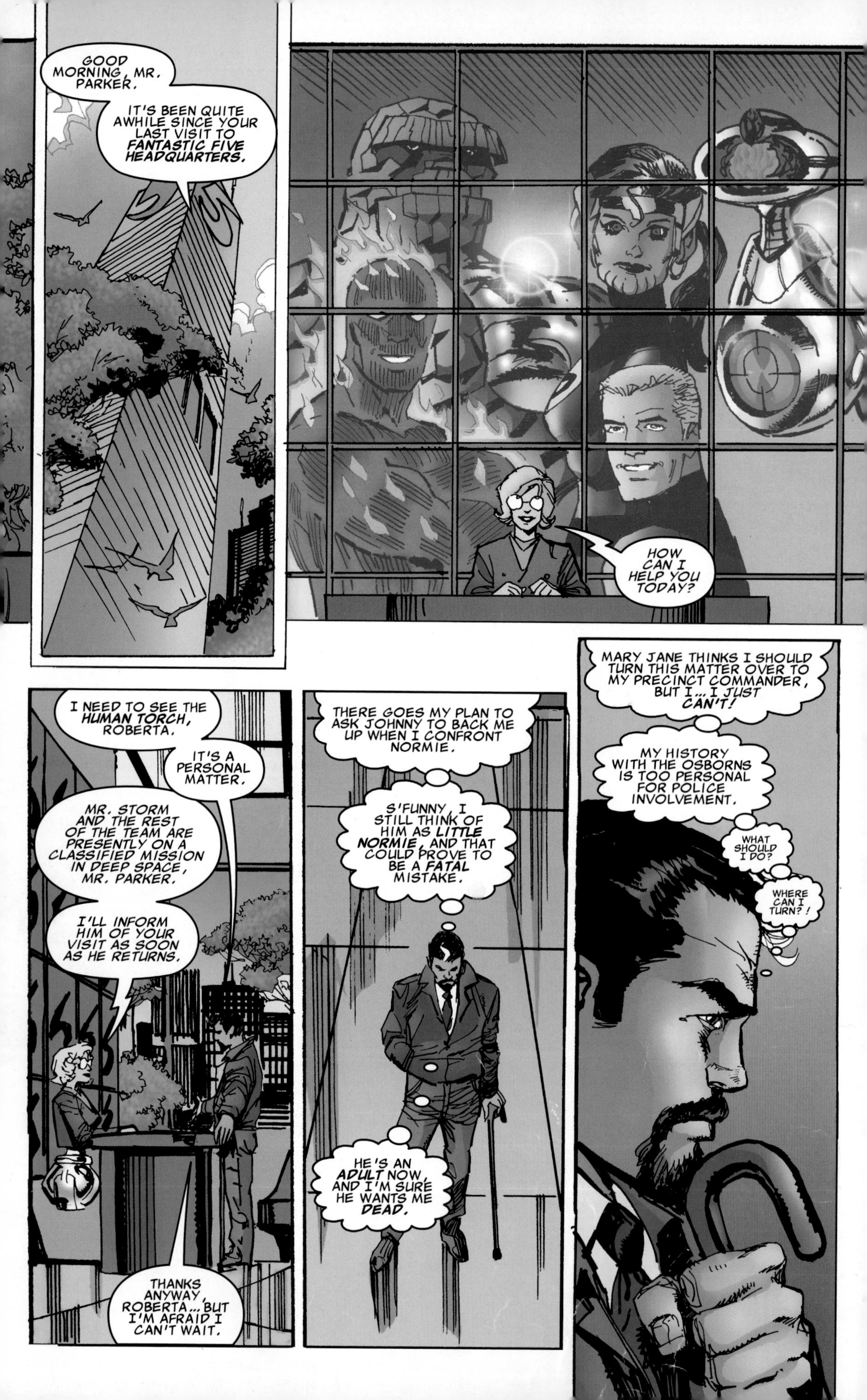
GOOD MORNING, MR. PARKER.
IT'S BEEN QUITE AWHILE SINCE YOUR LAST VISIT TO FANTASTIC FIVE HEADQUARTERS.
HOW CAN I HELP YOU TODAY?
I NEED TO SEE THE HUMAN TORCH, ROBERTA.
IT'S A PERSONAL MATTER.
MR. STORM AND THE REST OF THE TEAM ARE PRESENTLY ON A CLASSIFIED MISSION IN DEEP SPACE, MR. PARKER.
I'LL INFORM HIM OF YOUR VISIT AS SOON AS HE RETURNS.
THANKS ANYWAY, ROBERTA... BUT I'M AFRAID I CAN'T WAIT.
THERE GOES MY PLAN TO ASK JOHNNY TO BACK ME UP WHEN I CONFRONT NORMIE.
S'FUNNY, I STILL THINK OF HIM AS LITTLE NORMIE, AND THAT COULD PROVE TO BE A FATAL MISTAKE.
HE'S AN ADULT NOW, AND I'M SURE HE WANTS ME DEAD.
MARY JANE THINKS I SHOULD TURN THIS MATTER OVER TO MY PRECINCT COMMANDER, BUT I... I JUST CAN'T!
MY HISTORY WITH THE OSBORNS IS TOO PERSONAL FOR POLICE INVOLVEMENT.
WHAT SHOULD I DO?
WHERE CAN I TURN?!

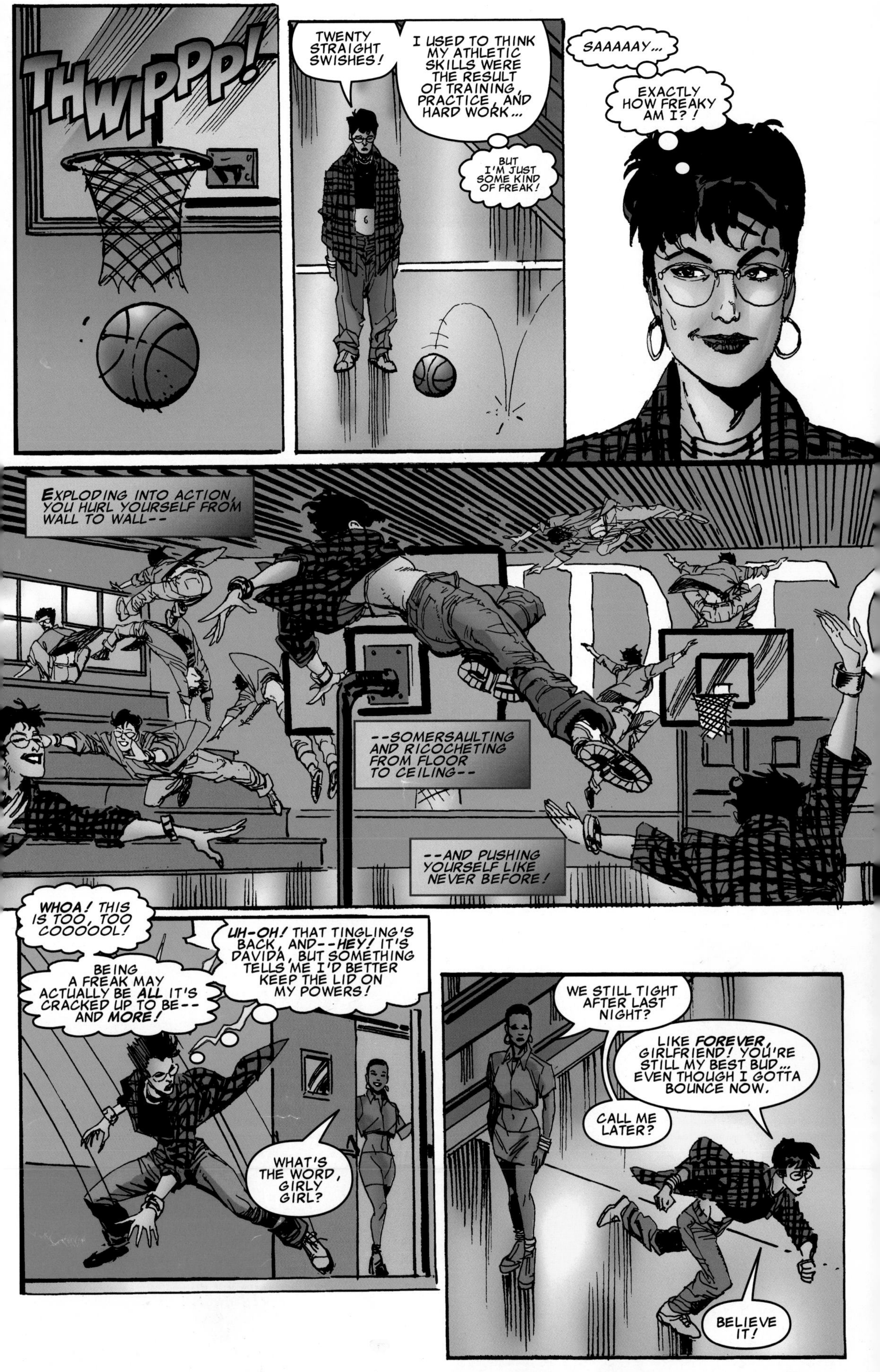
THWIPPP!
TWENTY STRAIGHT SWISHES!
I USED TO THINK MY ATHLETIC SKILLS WERE THE RESULT OF TRAINING, PRACTICE, AND HARD WORK...
BUT I'M JUST SOME KIND OF FREAK!
SAAAAAY...
EXACTLY HOW FREAKY AM I?!
EXPLODING INTO ACTION, YOU HURL YOURSELF FROM WALL TO WALL--
--SOMERSAULTING AND RICOCHETING FROM FLOOR TO CEILING--
--AND PUSHING YOURSELF LIKE NEVER BEFORE!
WHOA! THIS IS TOO, TOO COOOOOL!
BEING A FREAK MAY ACTUALLY BE ALL IT'S CRACKED UP TO BE--AND MORE!
UH-OH! THAT TINGLING'S BACK, AND--HEY! IT'S DAVIDA, BUT SOMETHING TELLS ME I'D BETTER KEEP THE LID ON MY POWERS!
WHAT'S THE WORD, GIRLY GIRL?
WE STILL TIGHT AFTER LAST NIGHT?
LIKE FOREVER, GIRLFRIEND! YOU'RE STILL MY BEST BUD... EVEN THOUGH I GOTTA BOUNCE NOW.
CALL ME LATER?
BELIEVE IT!

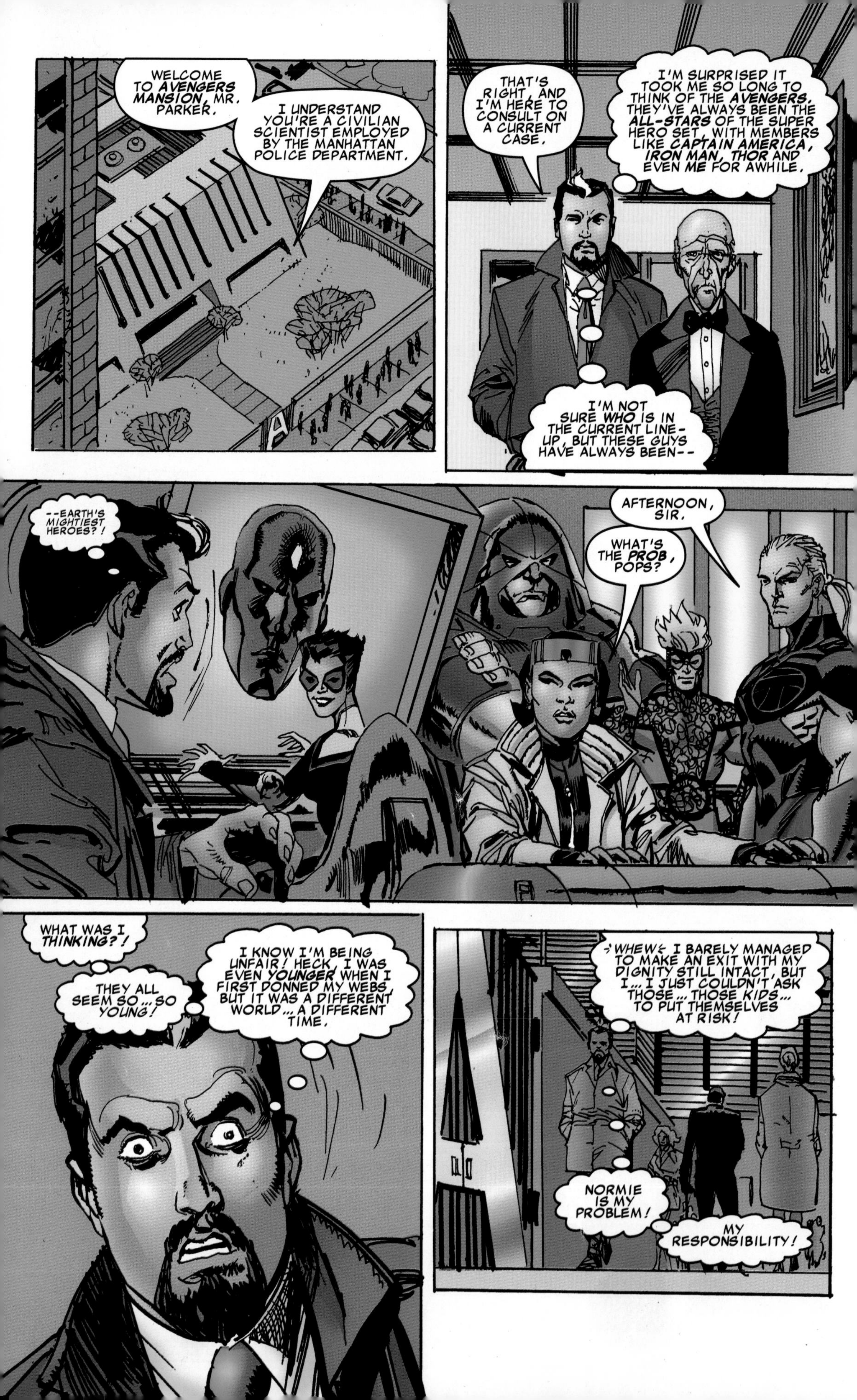
WELCOME TO AVENGERS MANSION, MR. PARKER.
I UNDERSTAND YOU'RE A CIVILIAN SCIENTIST EMPLOYED BY THE MANHATTAN POLICE DEPARTMENT.
THAT'S RIGHT, AND I'M HERE TO CONSULT ON A CURRENT CASE.
I'M SURPRISED IT TOOK ME SO LONG TO THINK OF THE AVENGERS. THEY'VE ALWAYS BEEN THE ALL-STARS OF THE SUPER HERO SET, WITH MEMBERS LIKE CAPTAIN AMERICA, IRON MAN, THOR AND EVEN ME FOR AWHILE.
I'M NOT SURE WHO IS IN THE CURRENT LINE-UP, BUT THESE GUYS HAVE ALWAYS BEEN--
--EARTH'S MIGHTIEST HEROES?!
AFTERNOON, SIR.
WHAT'S THE PROB, POPS?
WHAT WAS I THINKING?!
THEY ALL SEEM SO... SO YOUNG!
I KNOW I'M BEING UNFAIR! HECK, I WAS EVEN YOUNGER WHEN I FIRST DONNED MY WEBS, BUT IT WAS A DIFFERENT WORLD... A DIFFERENT TIME.
WHEW I BARELY MANAGED TO MAKE AN EXIT WITH MY DIGNITY STILL INTACT, BUT I... I JUST COULDN'T ASK THOSE... THOSE KIDS... TO PUT THEMSELVES AT RISK!
NORMIE IS MY PROBLEM!
MY RESPONSIBILITY!

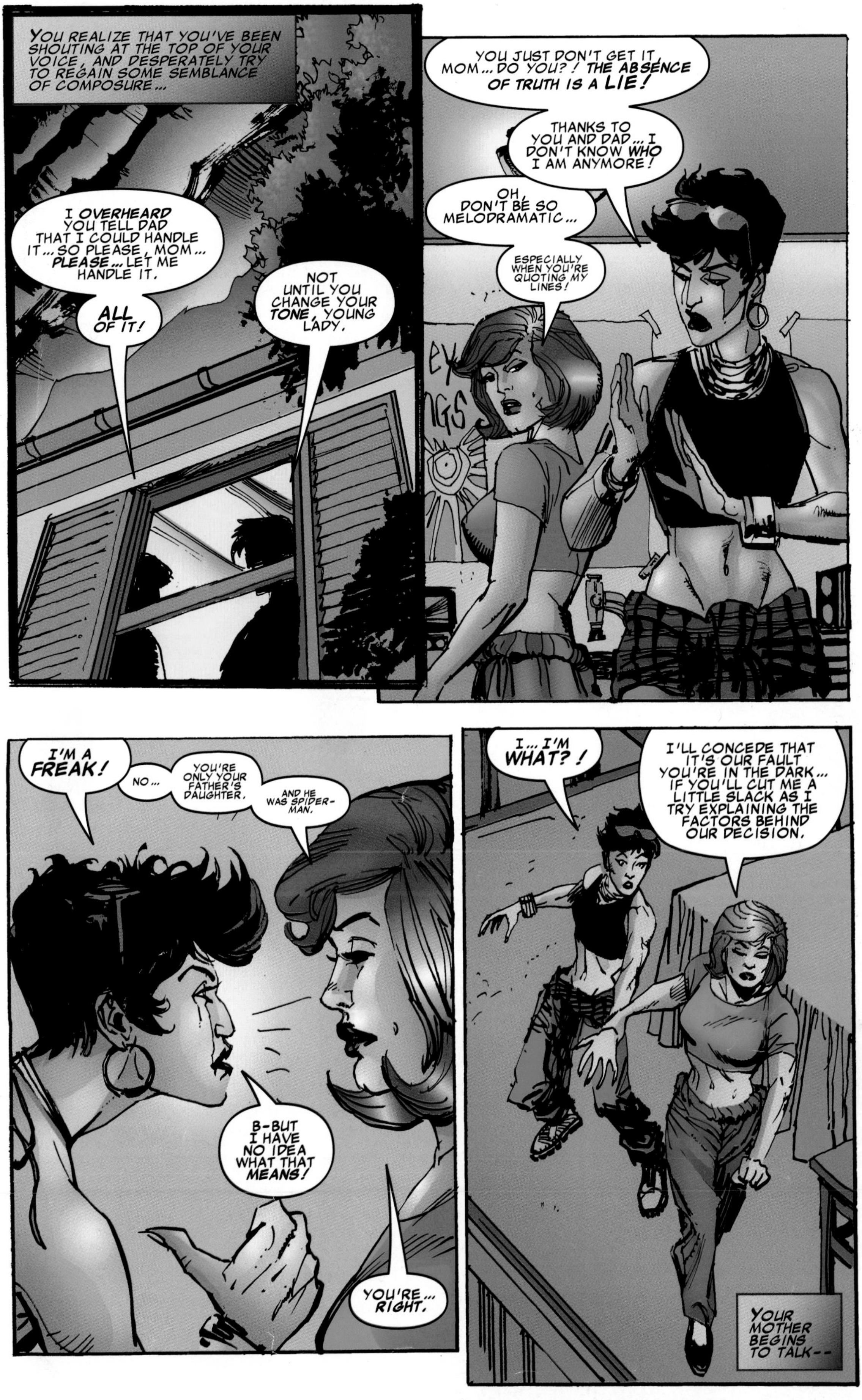
YOU REALIZE THAT YOU'VE BEEN SHOUTING AT THE TOP OF YOUR VOICE, AND DESPERATELY TRY TO REGAIN SOME SEMBLANCE OF COMPOSURE...
I OVERHEARD YOU TELL DAD THAT I COULD HANDLE IT... SO PLEASE, MOM... PLEASE... LET ME HANDLE IT.
ALL OF IT!
NOT UNTIL YOU CHANGE YOUR TONE, YOUNG LADY.
YOU JUST DON'T GET IT, MOM... DO YOU?! THE ABSENCE OF TRUTH IS A LIE!
THANKS TO YOU AND DAD... I DON'T KNOW WHO I AM ANYMORE!
OH, DON'T BE SO MELODRAMATIC...
ESPECIALLY WHEN YOU'RE QUOTING MY LINES!
I'M A FREAK!
NO...
YOU'RE ONLY YOUR FATHER'S DAUGHTER.
AND HE WAS SPIDER-MAN.
B-BUT I HAVE NO IDEA WHAT THAT MEANS!
YOU'RE... RIGHT.
I... I'M WHAT?!
I'LL CONCEDE THAT IT'S OUR FAULT YOU'RE IN THE DARK... IF YOU'LL CUT ME A LITTLE SLACK AS I TRY EXPLAINING THE FACTORS BEHIND OUR DECISION.
YOUR MOTHER BEGINS TO TALK--

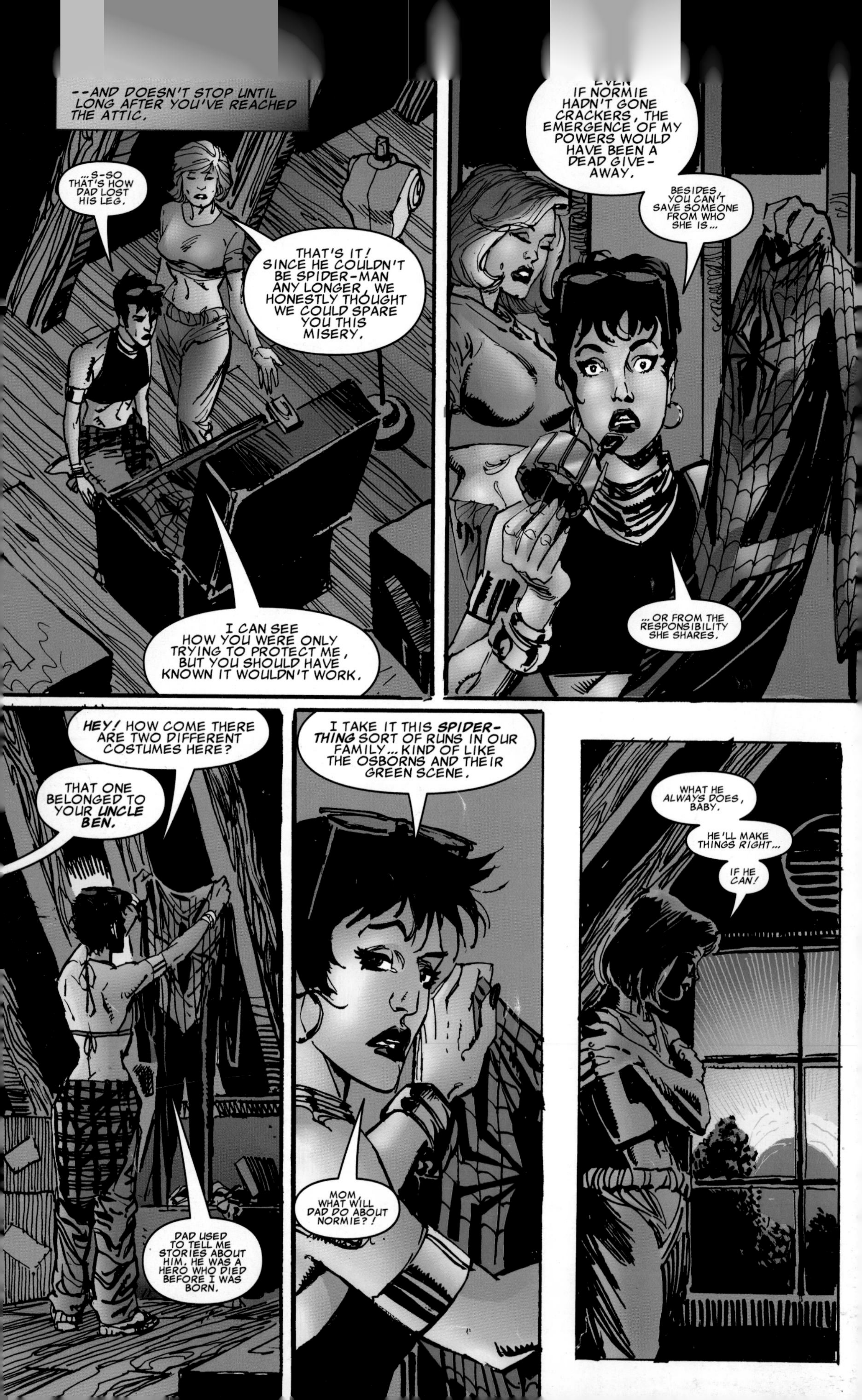
--AND DOESN'T STOP UNTIL LONG AFTER YOU'VE REACHED THE ATTIC.
...S-SO THAT'S HOW DAD LOST HIS LEG.
THAT'S IT! SINCE HE COULDN'T BE SPIDER-MAN ANY LONGER, WE HONESTLY THOUGHT WE COULD SPARE YOU THIS MISERY.
I CAN SEE HOW YOU WERE ONLY TRYING TO PROTECT ME, BUT YOU SHOULD HAVE KNOWN IT WOULDN'T WORK.
EVEN IF NORMIE HADN'T GONE CRACKERS, THE EMERGENCE OF MY POWERS WOULD HAVE BEEN A DEAD GIVE-AWAY.
BESIDES, YOU CAN'T SAVE SOMEONE FROM WHO SHE IS...
...OR FROM THE RESPONSIBILITY SHE SHARES.
HEY! HOW COME THERE ARE TWO DIFFERENT COSTUMES HERE?
THAT ONE BELONGED TO YOUR UNCLE BEN.
DAD USED TO TELL ME STORIES ABOUT HIM. HE WAS A HERO WHO DIED BEFORE I WAS BORN.
I TAKE IT THIS SPIDER-THING SORT OF RUNS IN OUR FAMILY... KIND OF LIKE THE OSBORNS AND THEIR GREEN SCENE.
MOM, WHAT WILL DAD DO ABOUT NORMIE?!
WHAT HE ALWAYS DOES, BABY.
HE'LL MAKE THINGS RIGHT...
IF HE CAN!

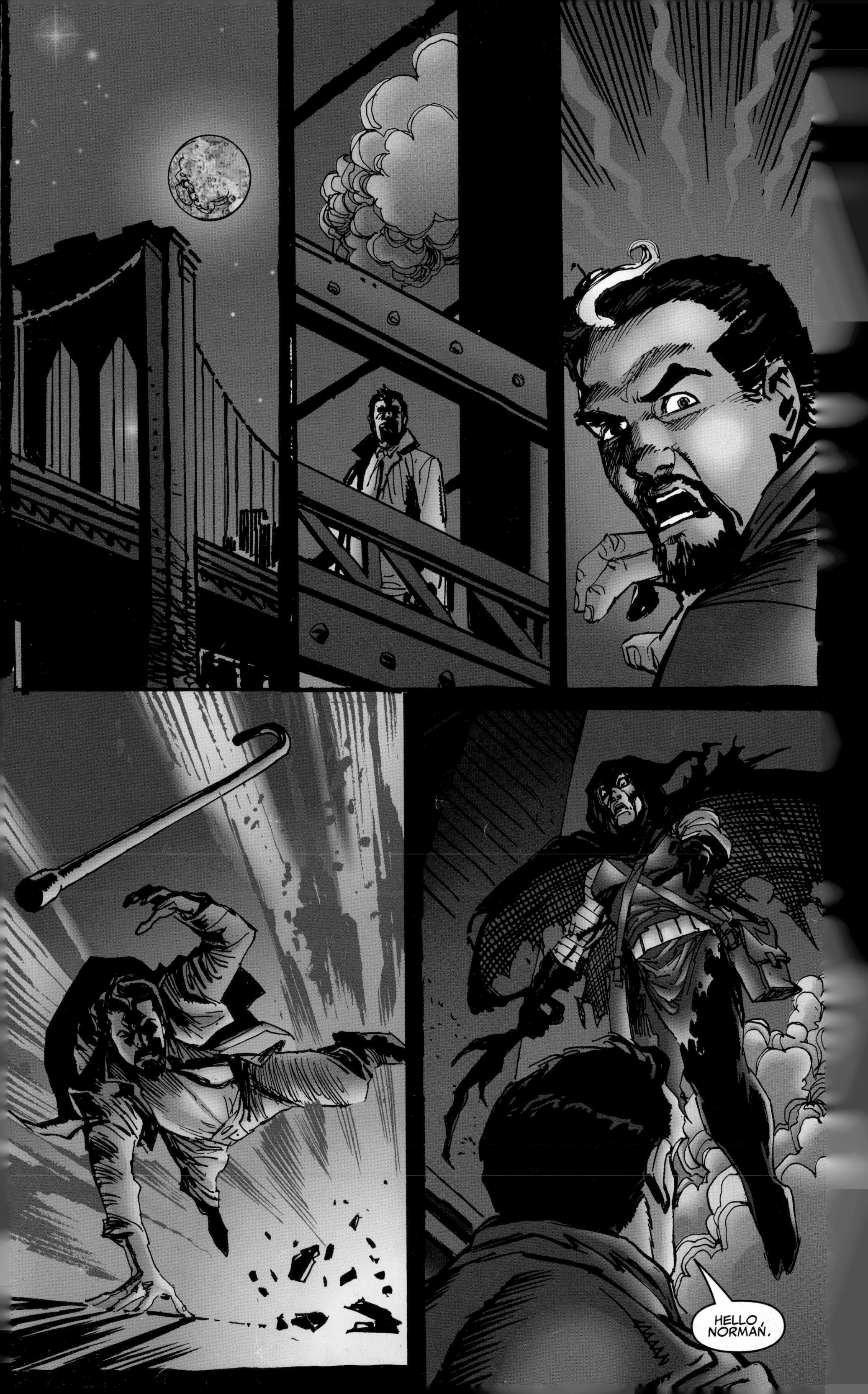
HELLO, NORMAN.

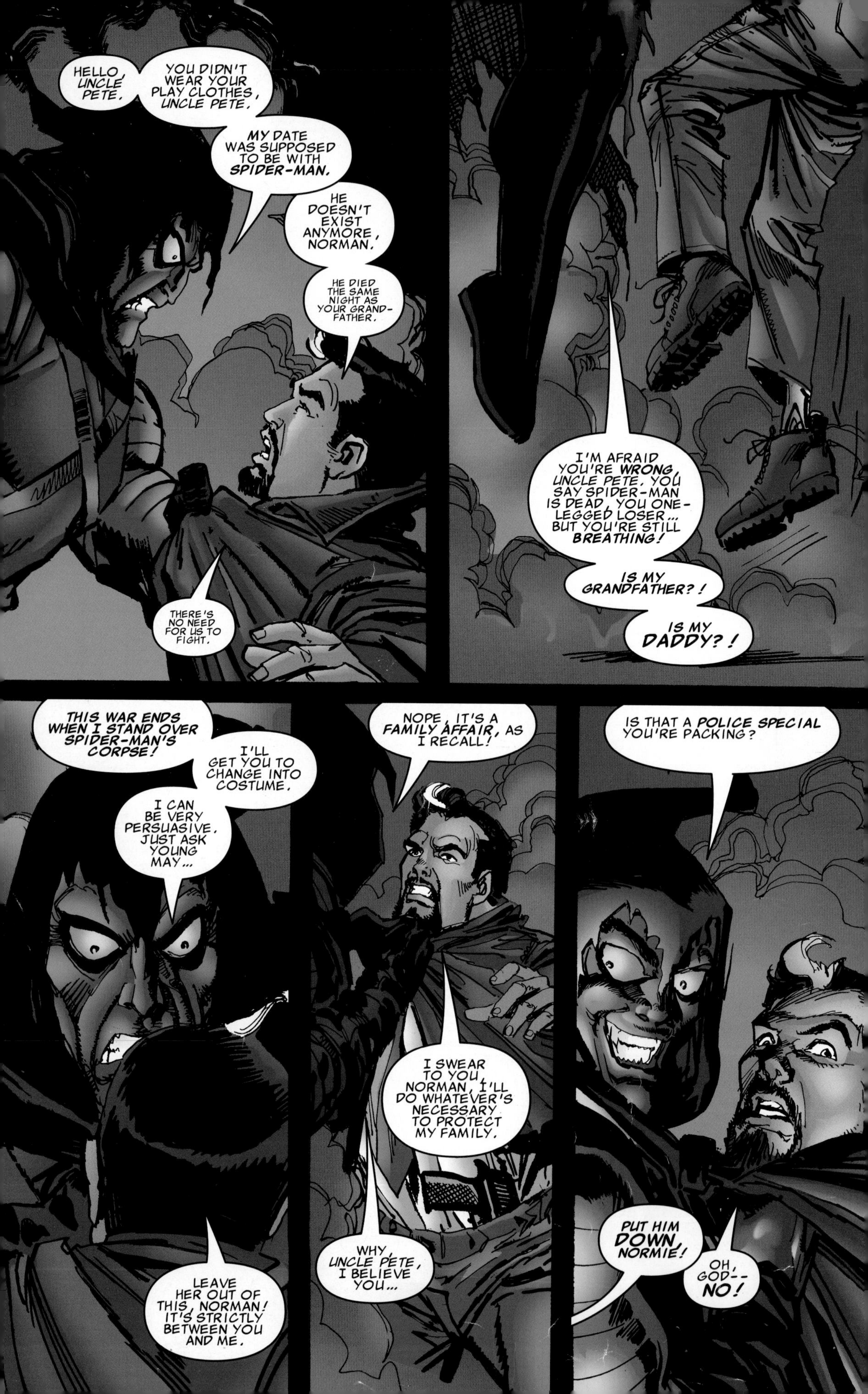
HELLO, UNCLE PETE.
YOU DIDN'T WEAR YOUR PLAY CLOTHES, UNCLE PETE.
MY DATE WAS SUPPOSED TO BE WITH SPIDER-MAN.
HE DOESN'T EXIST ANYMORE, NORMAN.
HE DIED THE SAME NIGHT AS YOUR GRAND-FATHER.
THERE'S NO NEED FOR US TO FIGHT.
I'M AFRAID YOU'RE WRONG, UNCLE PETE. YOU SAY SPIDER-MAN IS DEAD, YOU ONE-LEGGED LOSER... BUT YOU'RE STILL BREATHING!
IS MY GRANDFATHER?!
IS MY DADDY?!
THIS WAR ENDS WHEN I STAND OVER SPIDER-MAN'S CORPSE!
I'LL GET YOU TO CHANGE INTO COSTUME.
I CAN BE VERY PERSUASIVE. JUST ASK YOUNG MAY...
LEAVE HER OUT OF THIS, NORMAN! IT'S STRICTLY BETWEEN YOU AND ME.
NOPE, IT'S A FAMILY AFFAIR, AS I RECALL!
I SWEAR TO YOU, NORMAN, I'LL DO WHATEVER'S NECESSARY TO PROTECT MY FAMILY.
WHY, UNCLE PETE, I BELIEVE YOU...
IS THAT A POLICE SPECIAL YOU'RE PACKING?
PUT HIM DOWN, NORMIE!
OH, GOD-- NO!

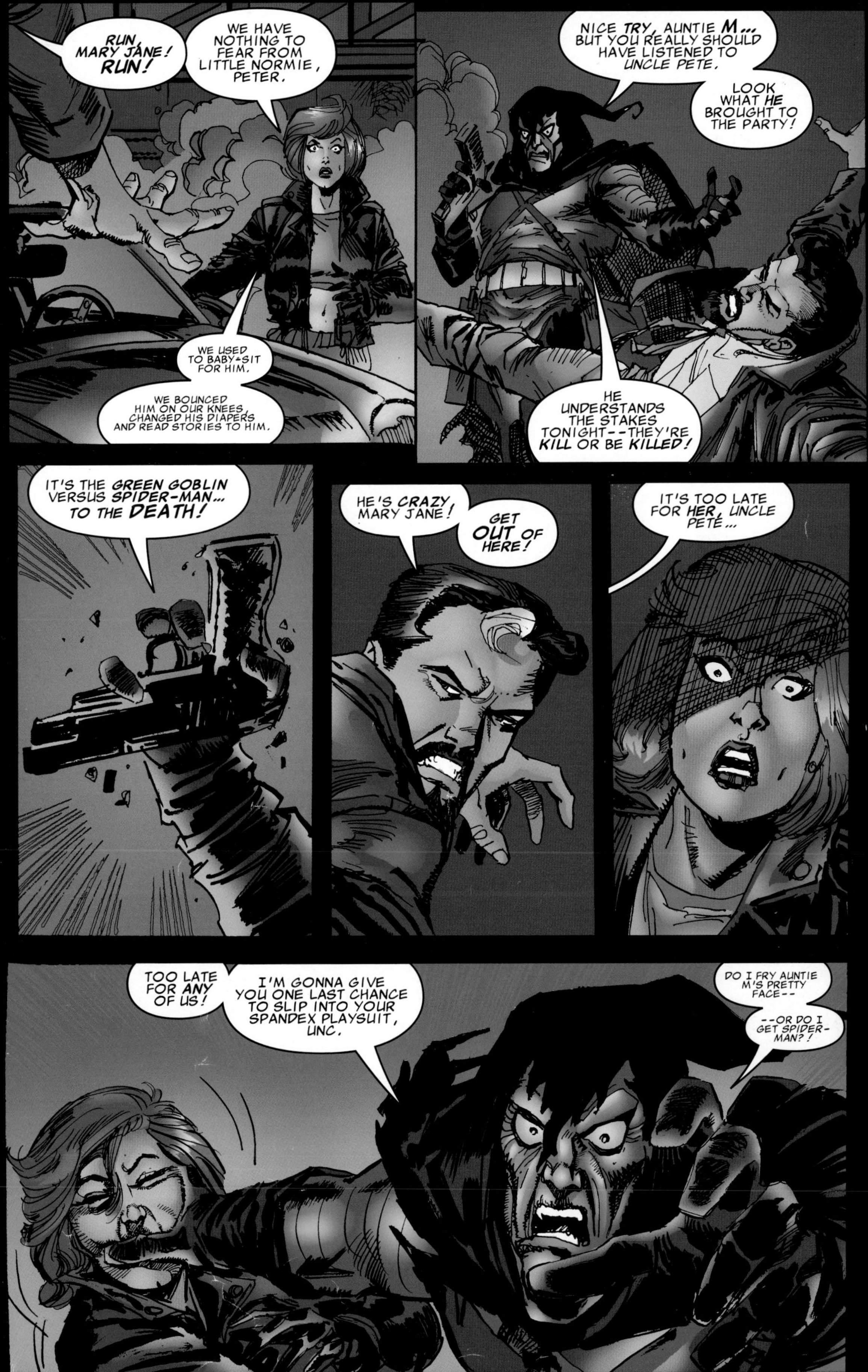
RUN, MARY JANE! RUN!
WE HAVE NOTHING TO FEAR FROM LITTLE NORMIE, PETER.
WE USED TO BABY-SIT FOR HIM.
WE BOUNCED HIM ON OUR KNEES, CHANGED HIS DIAPERS AND READ STORIES TO HIM.
NICE TRY, AUNTIE M... BUT YOU REALLY SHOULD HAVE LISTENED TO UNCLE PETE.
LOOK WHAT HE BROUGHT TO THE PARTY!
HE UNDERSTANDS THE STAKES TONIGHT--THEY'RE KILL OR BE KILLED!
IT'S THE GREEN GOBLIN VERSUS SPIDER-MAN... TO THE DEATH!
HE'S CRAZY, MARY JANE!
GET OUT OF HERE!
IT'S TOO LATE FOR HER, UNCLE PETE...
TOO LATE FOR ANY OF US!
I'M GONNA GIVE YOU ONE LAST CHANCE TO SLIP INTO YOUR SPANDEX PLAYSUIT, UNC.
DO I FRY AUNTIE M'S PRETTY FACE--
--OR DO I GET SPIDER-MAN?!

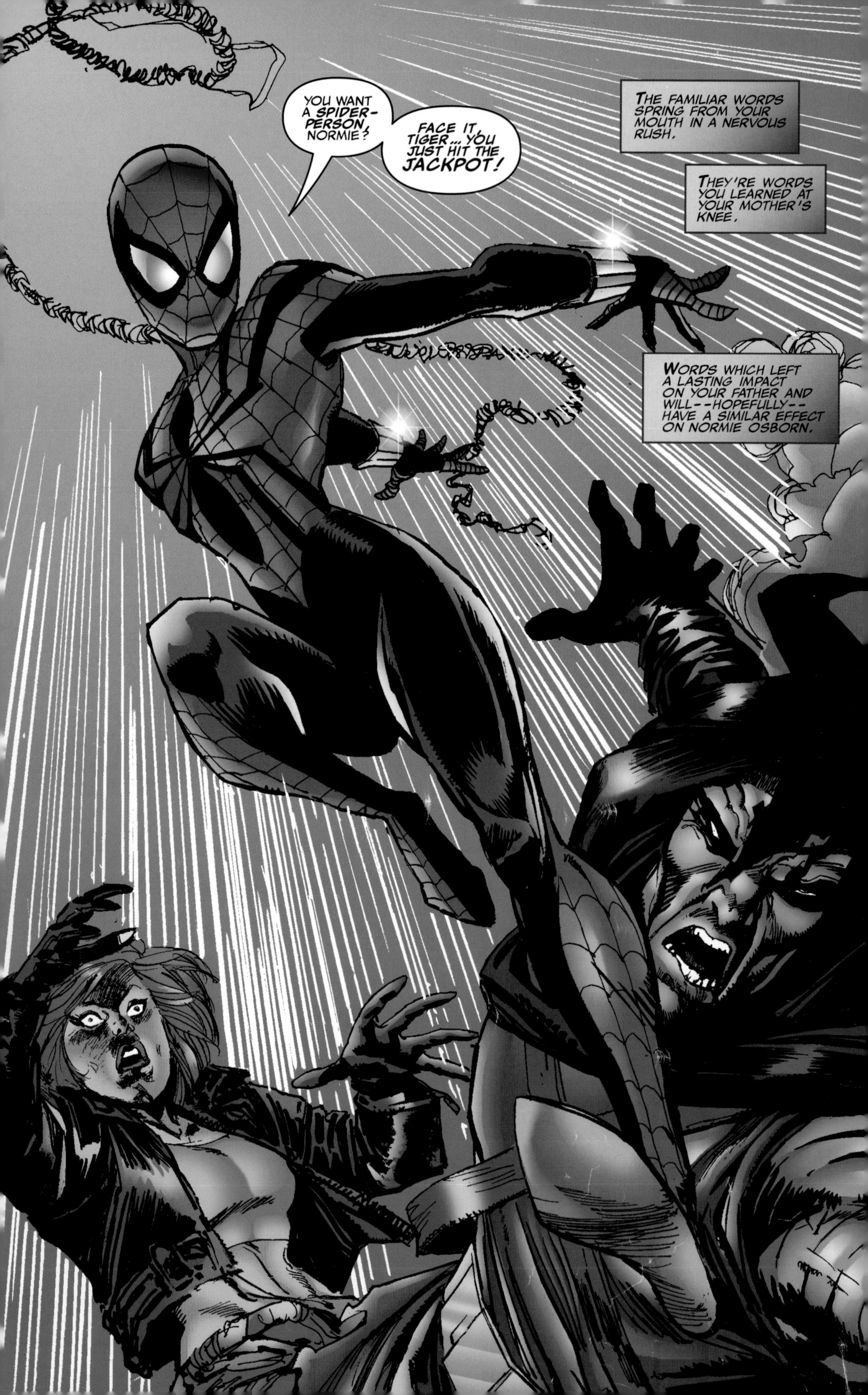
YOU WANT A SPIDER-PERSON, NORMIE?
FACE IT, TIGER... YOU JUST HIT THE JACKPOT!
THE FAMILIAR WORDS SPRING FROM YOUR MOUTH IN A NERVOUS RUSH.
THEY'RE WORDS YOU LEARNED AT YOUR MOTHER'S KNEE.
WORDS WHICH LEFT A LASTING IMPACT ON YOUR FATHER AND WILL--HOPEFULLY--HAVE A SIMILAR EFFECT ON NORMIE OSBORN.

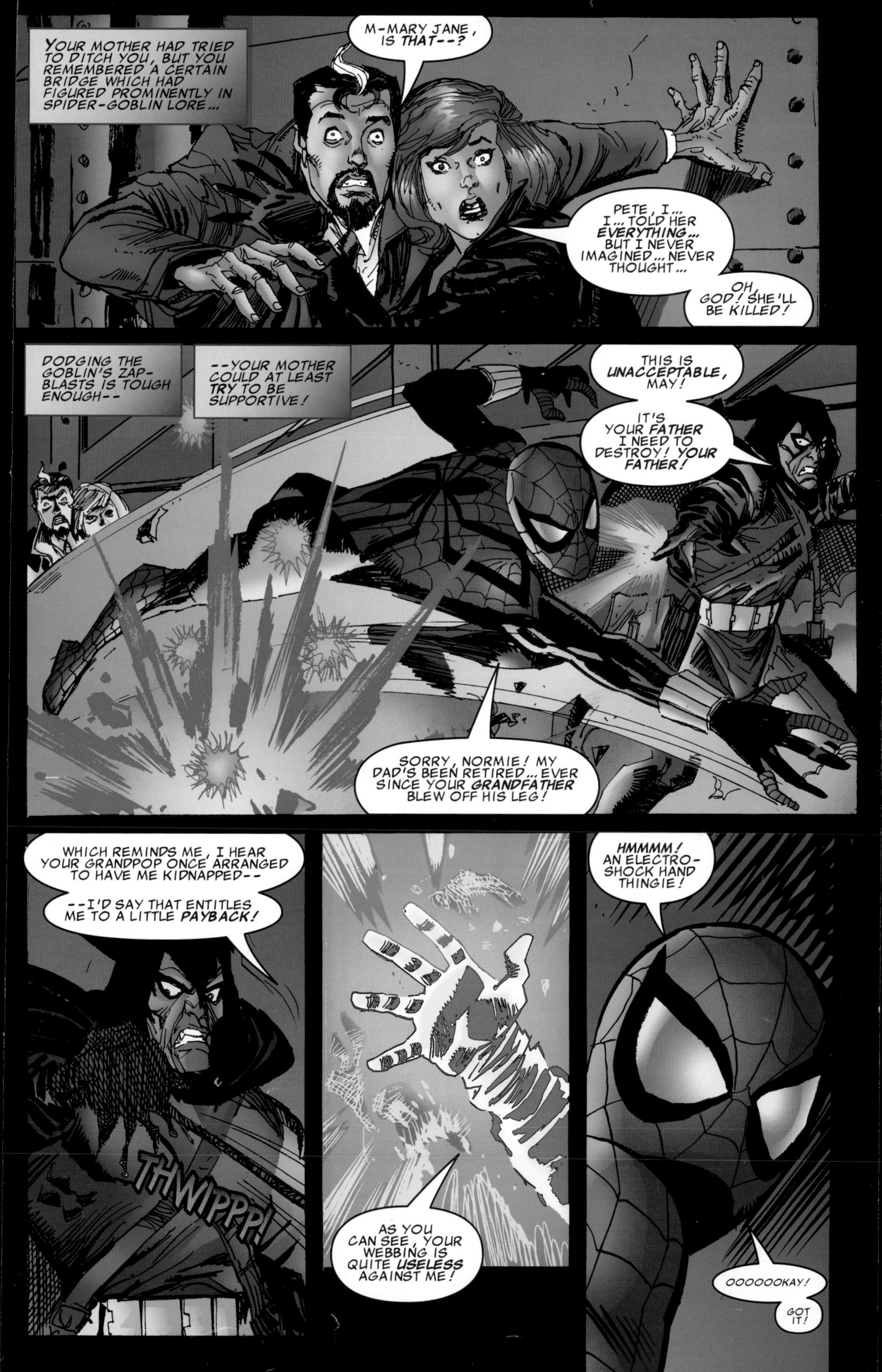

YOUR MOTHER HAD TRIED TO DITCH YOU, BUT YOU REMEMBERED A CERTAIN BRIDGE WHICH HAD FIGURED PROMINENTLY IN SPIDER-GOBLIN LORE...
M-MARY JANE, IS THAT--?
PETE, I... I... TOLD HER EVERYTHING... BUT I NEVER IMAGINED... NEVER THOUGHT...
OH, GOD! SHE'LL BE KILLED!
DODGING THE GOBLIN'S ZAP-BLASTS IS TOUGH ENOUGH--
--YOUR MOTHER COULD AT LEAST TRY TO BE SUPPORTIVE!
THIS IS UNACCEPTABLE, MAY!
IT'S YOUR FATHER I NEED TO DESTROY! YOUR FATHER!
SORRY, NORMIE! MY DAD'S BEEN RETIRED... EVER SINCE YOUR GRANDFATHER BLEW OFF HIS LEG!
WHICH REMINDS ME, I HEAR YOUR GRANDPOP ONCE ARRANGED TO HAVE ME KIDNAPPED--
--I'D SAY THAT ENTITLES ME TO A LITTLE PAYBACK!
THWIPPP!
AS YOU CAN SEE, YOUR WEBBING IS QUITE USELESS AGAINST ME!
HMMMM! AN ELECTRO-SHOCK HAND THINGIE!
OOOOOOKAY!
GOT IT!

YOU ALMOST GASP IN WONDER AS YOU ACTUALLY FIND YOURSELF *STICKING* TO AND *RUNNING* UP THE BRIDGE'S LOWER CORD...

YOU WERE OLDER, NORMIE... BUT WE SOMETIMES PLAYED TOGETHER AS KIDS.

WHY ARE YOU GUNNING FOR MY DAD? WHAT'S YOUR MAJOR *MAD-ON*?!

INJUSTICES MUST BE RIGHTED, YOUNG MAY! AGONIES MUST BE PAID IN KIND!

YOU MIND BEING A WEEEE BIT MORE SPECIFIC?!

S-SHE'S DOING *WELL*--KEEPING HIM TALKING AND OFF-BALANCE!

B-BUT SHE'S TOO *YOUNG*--TOO INEXPERIENCED!

I REALLY WOULD HAVE TRIED TO SPARE YOU AND AUNTIE M, BUT YOU'VE GIVEN ME *NO* CHOICE!

YOU'RE GOING TO *DIE*, LITTLE SPIDER-GIRL!

LIKE MY *GRANDFATHER!*

LIKE MY OWN *FATHER!*

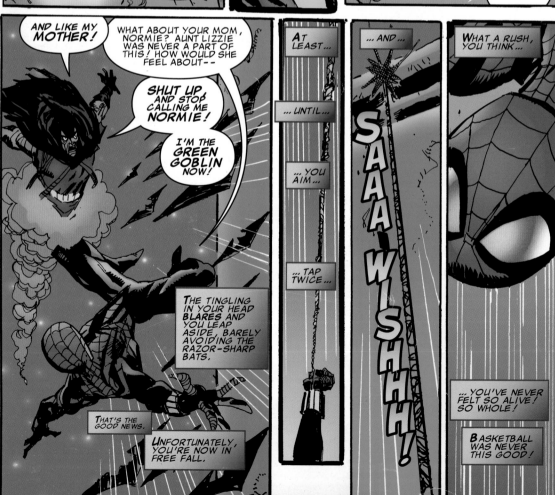

AND LIKE MY *MOTHER!*

WHAT ABOUT YOUR MOM, NORMIE? AUNT LIZZIE WAS NEVER A PART OF THIS! HOW WOULD SHE FEEL ABOUT--

SHUT UP AND STOP CALLING ME *NORMIE!*

I'M THE *GREEN GOBLIN* NOW!

THE TINGLING IN YOUR HEAD BLARES AND YOU LEAP ASIDE, BARELY AVOIDING THE RAZOR-SHARP BATS.

THAT'S THE GOOD NEWS.

UNFORTUNATELY, YOU'RE NOW IN FREE FALL.

AT LEAST...

...UNTIL...

...YOU AIM...

...TAP TWICE...

...AND...

SAAAWISHH!

WHAT A RUSH, YOU THINK...

...YOU'VE NEVER FELT SO ALIVE! SO WHOLE!

BASKETBALL WAS NEVER THIS GOOD!

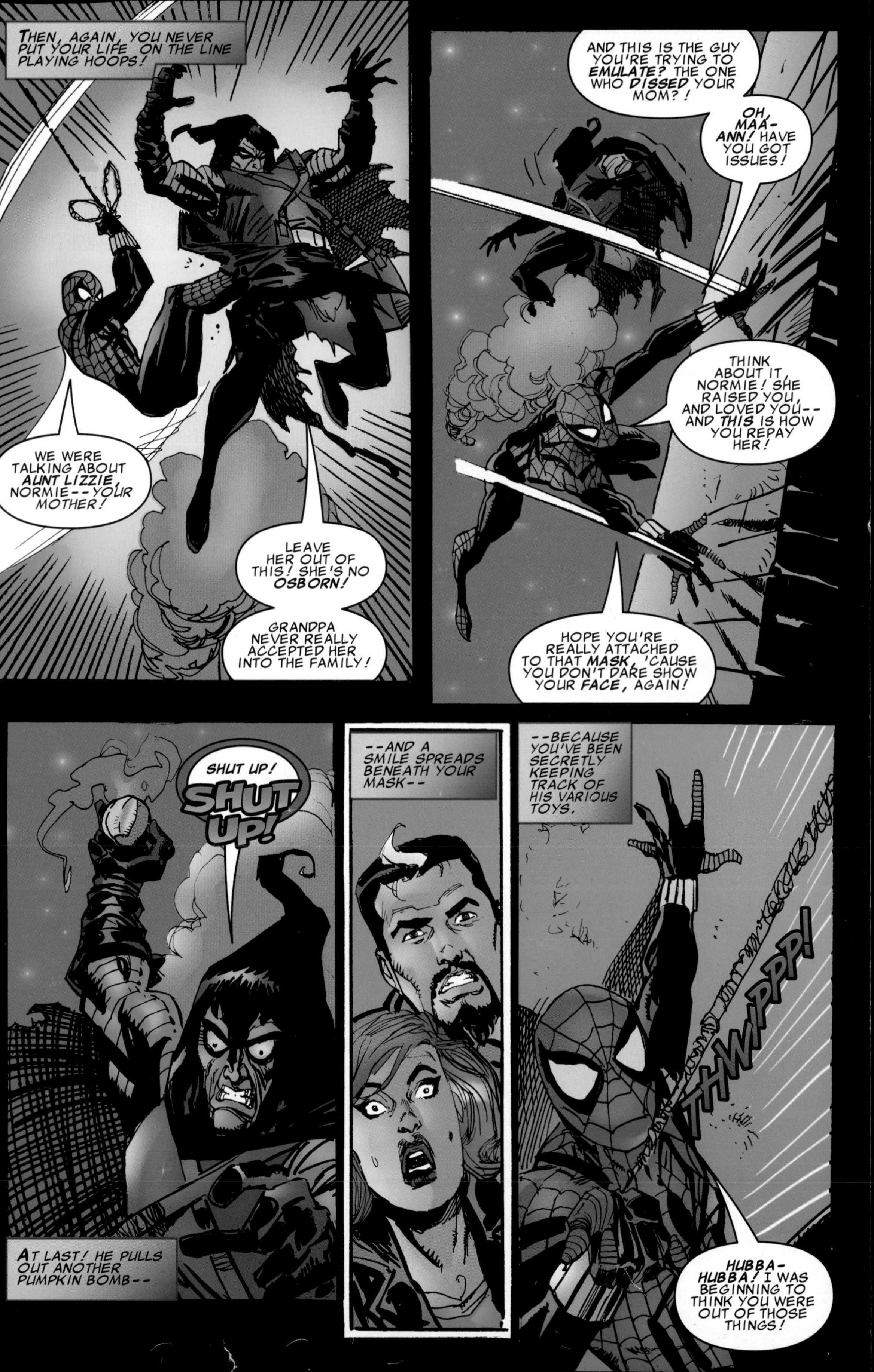
THEN, AGAIN, YOU NEVER PUT YOUR LIFE ON THE LINE PLAYING HOOPS!
WE WERE TALKING ABOUT AUNT LIZZIE, NORMIE--YOUR MOTHER!
LEAVE HER OUT OF THIS! SHE'S NO OSBORN!
GRANDPA NEVER REALLY ACCEPTED HER INTO THE FAMILY!
AND THIS IS THE GUY YOU'RE TRYING TO EMULATE? THE ONE WHO DISSED YOUR MOM?!
OH, MAA-ANN! HAVE YOU GOT ISSUES!
THINK ABOUT IT, NORMIE! SHE RAISED YOU, AND LOVED YOU--AND THIS IS HOW YOU REPAY HER!
HOPE YOU'RE REALLY ATTACHED TO THAT MASK, 'CAUSE YOU DON'T DARE SHOW YOUR FACE, AGAIN!
SHUT UP!
SHUT UP!
AT LAST! HE PULLS OUT ANOTHER PUMPKIN BOMB--
--AND A SMILE SPREADS BENEATH YOUR MASK--
--BECAUSE YOU'VE BEEN SECRETLY KEEPING TRACK OF HIS VARIOUS TOYS.
THWIPPP!
HUBBA-HUBBA! I WAS BEGINNING TO THINK YOU WERE OUT OF THOSE THINGS!

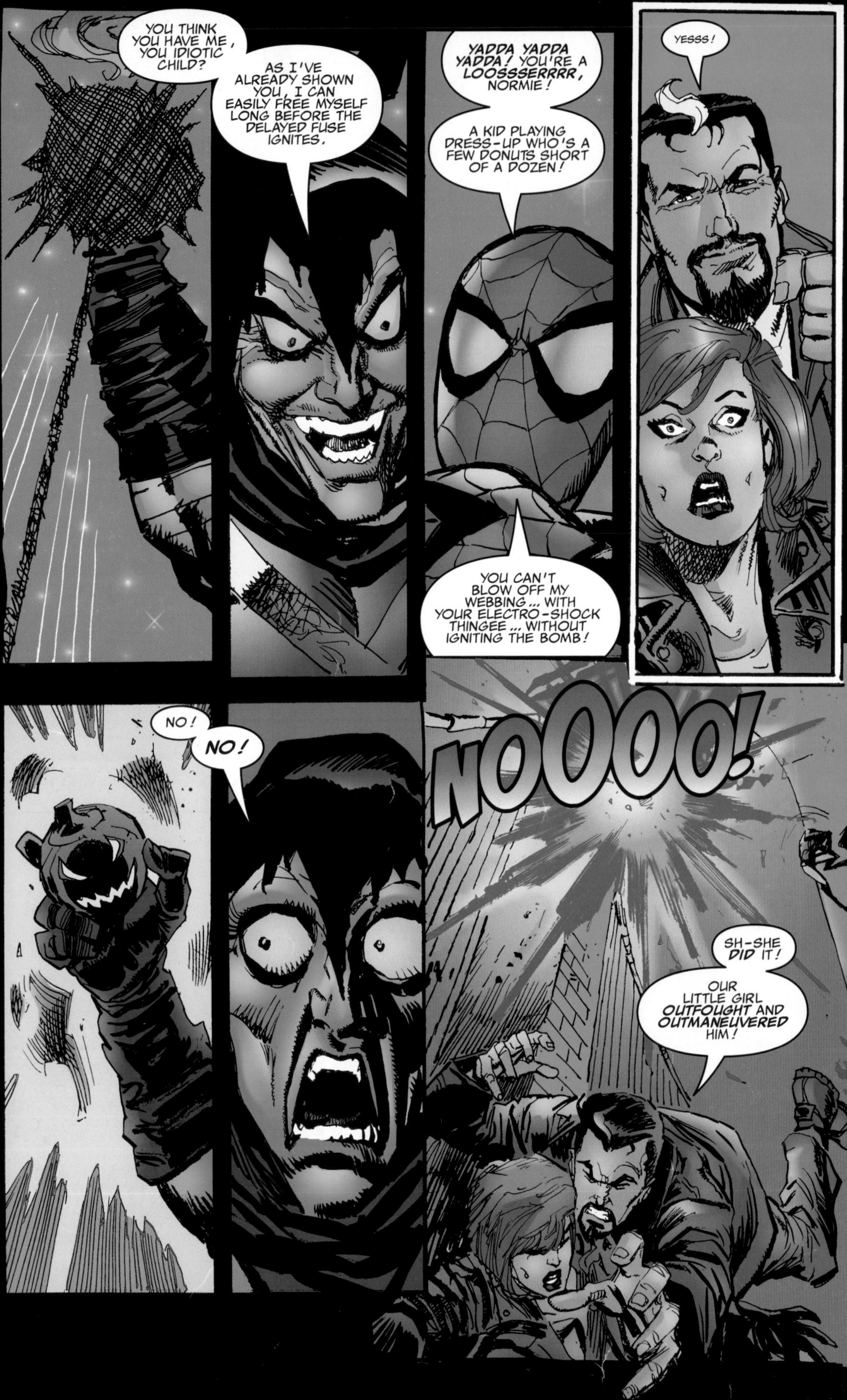
YOU THINK YOU HAVE ME, YOU IDIOTIC CHILD?
AS I'VE ALREADY SHOWN YOU, I CAN EASILY FREE MYSELF LONG BEFORE THE DELAYED FUSE IGNITES.
YADDA YADDA YADDA! YOU'RE A LOOSSSERRRR, NORMIE!
A KID PLAYING DRESS-UP WHO'S A FEW DONUTS SHORT OF A DOZEN!
YOU CAN'T BLOW OFF MY WEBBING... WITH YOUR ELECTRO-SHOCK THINGEE ... WITHOUT IGNITING THE BOMB!
YESSS!
NO!
NO!
NOOOO!
SH-SHE DID IT!
OUR LITTLE GIRL OUTFOUGHT AND OUTMANEUVERED HIM!

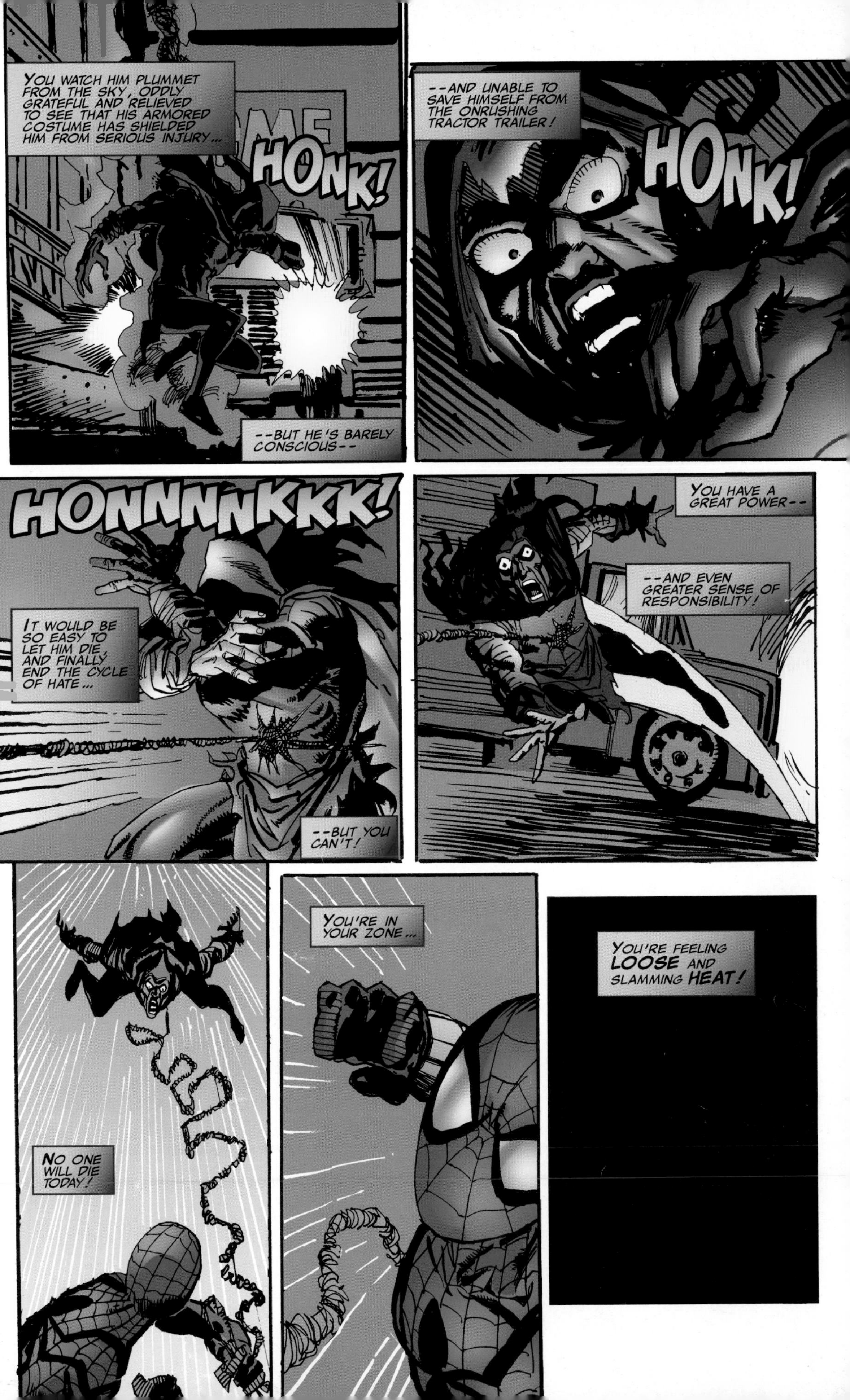
YOU WATCH HIM PLUMMET FROM THE SKY, ODDLY GRATEFUL AND RELIEVED TO SEE THAT HIS ARMORED COSTUME HAS SHIELDED HIM FROM SERIOUS INJURY...
HONK!
--BUT HE'S BARELY CONSCIOUS--
--AND UNABLE TO SAVE HIMSELF FROM THE ONRUSHING TRACTOR TRAILER!
HONK!
HONNNNKKK!
IT WOULD BE SO EASY TO LET HIM DIE, AND FINALLY END THE CYCLE OF HATE...
--BUT YOU CAN'T!
YOU HAVE A GREAT POWER--
--AND EVEN GREATER SENSE OF RESPONSIBILITY!
NO ONE WILL DIE TODAY!
YOU'RE IN YOUR ZONE...
YOU'RE FEELING LOOSE AND SLAMMING HEAT!

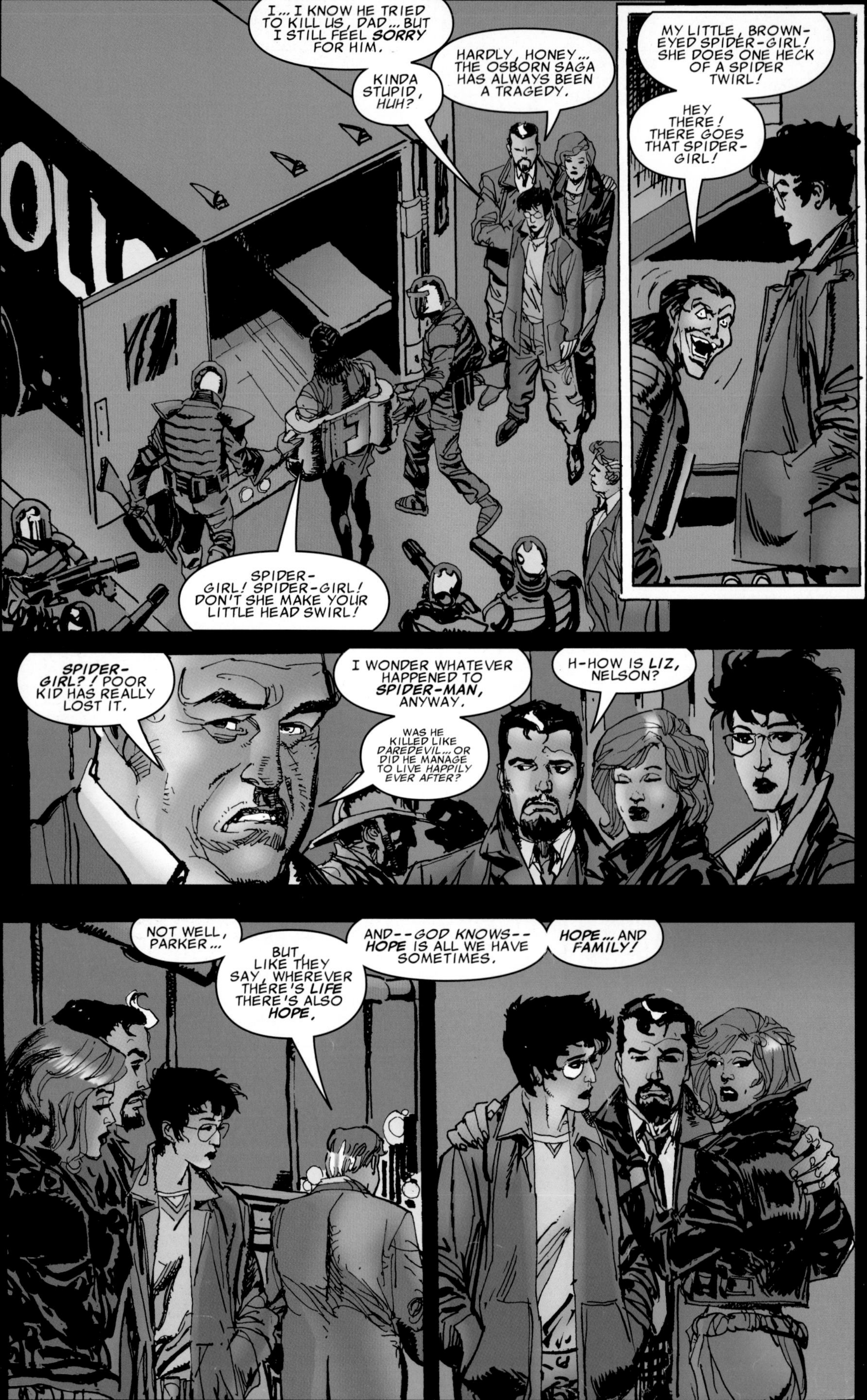
I... I KNOW HE TRIED TO KILL US, DAD... BUT I STILL FEEL SORRY FOR HIM.
KINDA STUPID, HUH?
HARDLY, HONEY... THE OSBORN SAGA HAS ALWAYS BEEN A TRAGEDY.
SPIDER-GIRL! SPIDER-GIRL! DON'T SHE MAKE YOUR LITTLE HEAD SWIRL!
MY LITTLE, BROWN-EYED SPIDER-GIRL! SHE DOES ONE HECK OF A SPIDER TWIRL!
HEY THERE! THERE GOES THAT SPIDER-GIRL!
SPIDER-GIRL?! POOR KID HAS REALLY LOST IT.
I WONDER WHATEVER HAPPENED TO SPIDER-MAN, ANYWAY.
WAS HE KILLED LIKE DAREDEVIL... OR DID HE MANAGE TO LIVE HAPPILY EVER AFTER?
H-HOW IS LIZ, NELSON?
NOT WELL, PARKER...
BUT, LIKE THEY SAY, WHEREVER THERE'S LIFE THERE'S ALSO HOPE.
AND--GOD KNOWS--HOPE IS ALL WE HAVE SOMETIMES.
HOPE... AND FAMILY!

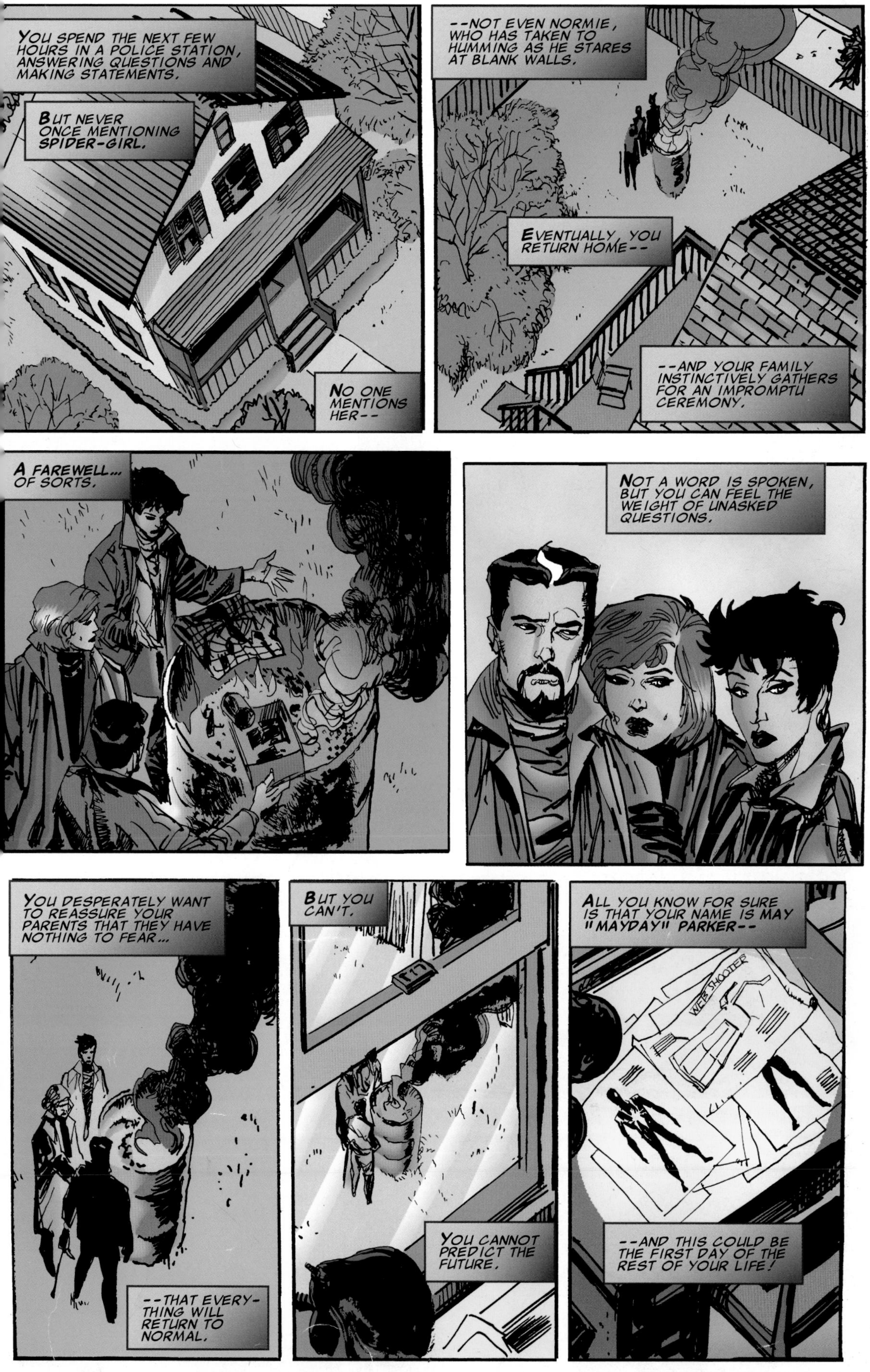
YOU SPEND THE NEXT FEW HOURS IN A POLICE STATION, ANSWERING QUESTIONS AND MAKING STATEMENTS.
BUT NEVER ONCE MENTIONING SPIDER-GIRL.
NO ONE MENTIONS HER--
--NOT EVEN NORMIE, WHO HAS TAKEN TO HUMMING AS HE STARES AT BLANK WALLS.
EVENTUALLY, YOU RETURN HOME--
--AND YOUR FAMILY INSTINCTIVELY GATHERS FOR AN IMPROMPTU CEREMONY.
A FAREWELL... OF SORTS.
NOT A WORD IS SPOKEN, BUT YOU CAN FEEL THE WEIGHT OF UNASKED QUESTIONS.
YOU DESPERATELY WANT TO REASSURE YOUR PARENTS THAT THEY HAVE NOTHING TO FEAR...
--THAT EVERY-THING WILL RETURN TO NORMAL.
BUT YOU CAN'T.
YOU CANNOT PREDICT THE FUTURE.
ALL YOU KNOW FOR SURE IS THAT YOUR NAME IS MAY "MAYDAY" PARKER--
WEB SHOOTER
--AND THIS COULD BE THE FIRST DAY OF THE REST OF YOUR LIFE!

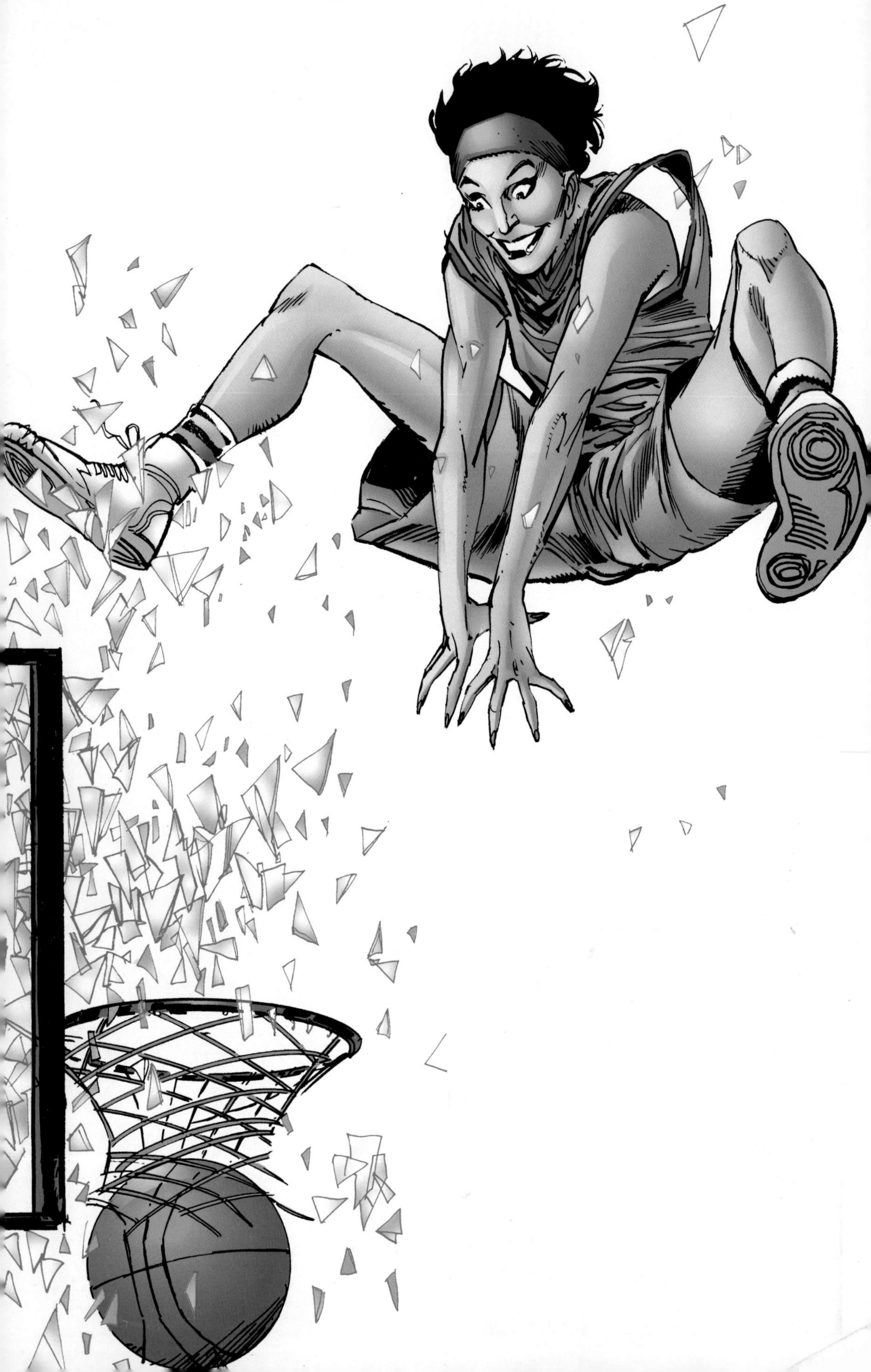